OMINOUS MIDSUMMER

Book 6 of Northern Shore Intrigue Series

LYN COTE

Chapter 1

He brought me up also out of a horrible pit,
out of the miry clay,
and set my feet upon a rock… Psalm 40:2 KJV

July 10th

Wearing hip boots and a wide-brimmed tan hat and holding a fly rod had become Jessie's favorite way to be. Under the warming early July sun, she let the gentle blue water of the cool stream flowing around her legs work its magic on her. The breeze ruffled the high leaves in the tall trees around, sounding like gentle laughter.

But now there was a problem, the same one she'd had repeatedly today. She sighed. She'd hooked another "brookie," wriggling to get free from her hand. She needed to release this baby trout to go on growing. But the hook wouldn't come out, and the fish was wriggling way more than usual. Then somehow it leaped from her water-slick hands back into the creek.

She again began drawing in the fish. "Foolish fish." She voiced her frustration. "I still have you hooked." Once again, she drew him up out of the water. The brookie continued fighting hard, arching its little body and swinging its tail.

"Another brookie! A feisty one!" she called to Chad, similarly garbed, who was fly-fishing near her. He turned to look at her, his brow lifted quizzically and his mouth quirked into a half grin. He loved to tease her as the newbie fly-fisher. But they had a mutual goal: to catch a couple of good-sized brook trout for supper.

"Need help?" Chad called, already wading over to her, moving the water in waves and making a sloshing sound.

"Yeah," she said with disgust. "He's got a wild streak in him."

"It could be a her, you know. You got a wild streak." Grinning, Chad came abreast of her.

She liked it when Chad teased her, like the big brother she'd never had. He was a head taller than she, lean and muscular, but not a big man. A compact package so to speak, with dark hair and eyes and a tanned, agreeable face. Soon their hat brims met over the wriggling fish. "You hold 'em, Jess. I'll work the hook out."

For several seconds, the two stood almost nose-to-nose over the fish. Jessie smelled the water, that rich scent so hard to describe, and Chad's faint summer sweat. The day was warm, but the winter had been long. The sun on her back felt good.

Finally, Chad, the more experienced angler, managed to slide the barbed hook out with the least damage to the brookie's lip. She released the small slick body into the current and watched it swim away. "Thanks. I'm still getting the hang of this."

"It's all right," Chad said, grinning at her as if he'd just heard a joke, a really good one.

She wouldn't let him hold out on her. "What's funny?"

"Your nose. You got fish on it." He swiped his sleeve over her nose.

She laughed out loud. "So what else is new?"

Chuckling, Chad looked at the horizon, no doubt judging the time by where the sun sat now just drifting below the tree-tops. The tall, dark pines contrasted against the summer green of the maples. "I think we need to clean the two good-sized ones we got and get them home for supper. Uncle Dick said he's hungry for trout."

"Well, so am I," she agreed. But right then she felt a tug on her line. She drew the line taut so she didn't lose the fish, another trout, she hoped. She let the line in and out as she coaxed the trout toward her.

Chad stood ready with the net. Finally he scooped it up for her. "Hey! A big one! Yes!" The two of them high-fived, grinning from ear to ear. Her heart expanded. These quiet times with Chad filled some empty, sad places that lingered within her.

Soon they were side by side, wading out of the stream. On the grassy, somewhat rocky shore, they cleaned the three trout, leaving the discarded parts for the eagle that had appeared, swooping overhead and waiting for them to leave. They shed their waders and tossed them and their fishing gear into the back of Chad's vintage red Ford pickup. When Jessie settled on the seat, all the tension and excitement of fighting the last fish into the net left her. "I love fly-fishing," she said.

Chad chuckled. "And I'm glad to have a fishing buddy."

Jessie smiled. People were always trying to make her friend-ship with Chad into a romance, but it wasn't. He understood. He never crossed the line or even looked like he wanted to. He was a friend, her good friend. And that was all she could handle for now. Maybe ever.

Soon they drove up the county highway, hemmed in by the forest, and turned in at the lane that led to the old Blaney farmhouse. Dick Blaney was Chad's great uncle, and Chad's dad lived with him. Uncle Dick had a touchy heart and Chad's dad needed a home. The situation was good for both of them was the common judgment around Winfield, though some still had doubts. The grill was outside the garage as if in anticipation of their catch.

Chad tooted his horn as they drove up to the two-story white farmhouse. No one responded. After parking in the shade, Chad and Jessie got out of the truck. Chad carried the creel with the trout toward the garage. "Hey! Got the grill fired up?"

No answer.

The double garage door was up so they walked that way. Maybe Dick or Chad's dad was working on something in there or out back. And they could walk through the garage to—

At the garage entrance Jessie screamed. The sound echoed inside her like a shock wave. She jerked to a halt.

Chad rushed forward and dropped to his knees beside his white-haired great uncle. "He's bleeding!"

Jessie sprinted forward, breaking free. "Is he breathing?"

"Yeah." Chad was already pressing a finger to the man's neck, feeling for a pulse. "His heart's racing and the pulse doesn't feel strong. If he had another heart attack, why would he be bleeding? Did he hit his head when he fell?"

"Don't know." Her own pulse sped up, pounding in her ears. Jessie slipped out her cell and tapped in 911. She spoke as soon as the other party answered, "We need an ambulance at Dick Blaney's. Maybe a heart attack." She rattled off the address. "He's unconscious and bleeding. Hurry. Please." Ignoring the dispatcher's instruction to stay on the line, she cut off the call and dropped down on the cement floor on the opposite side of Dick, studying him. His head wound didn't look like he'd just taken a fall. Bruises were developing on his jaw and one eye was swelling, as if he'd been...struck. Icy fear zipped through her. She pressed down a swell of panic. *Think.* "You need to look for your dad," Jessie urged. "If he's here, he might be hurt too." What had happened here? "I'll stay with Dick. Help's on the way."

Chad surged to his feet and started calling, "Dad! Dad!" He ran out the back door of the garage into the yard.

The frantic edge to his voice destroyed the last shred of the peace Jessie had brought with her. She claimed Dick's hand and began praying help would come soon, come in time. *Please.*

She could hear Chad, still calling, "Dad! Dad!" She clung to Dick's large, rough hand as if she could hold on to him, keep him here. Then she heard Chad's voice coming from inside the house.

Chad burst back into the garage through the door connecting the garage and house. His hat had slid down, still held on the back of his neck by its string. His thick, dark hair stuck out like wild grass. "Something bad's happened!" He panted with exertion, his eyes wide. "The living room is torn up like there was a fight or something."

Jessie gasped. "Oh, no!" At this proof of violence, remembered terror tingled from her neck, down her arms. She shook it off, focused on Dick.

The sound of a siren broke into their exchange. "Go wave them in here," she said.

Chad left without another word.

She heard him telling the ambulance driver that Dick was in the garage. Help had come. She drew in a slow breath. Help had come.

Soon she moved back to let the EMTs take over and moved close to Chad. They stood shoulder to shoulder and she knew that he was praying too, because his lips were moving. *Lord, help Dick. Help my friend.*

———

GLAD TO HAVE Jessie beside him, Chad felt the surging panic rising in him. Not letting his mind take him where he didn't want to go, he squashed it down with all he was worth. *God, what happened here,* he begged. Nothing made sense. When he and Jessie had left to go angling in the nearby stream, everything had been normal. His dad and Uncle Dick were, as usual, bickering about whether they should try to plant a garden again this year. The year before deer and rabbits had "harvested" most of the vegetables. But Uncle Dick was sure they could figure out a fence that would protect their food, declaring he liked to pick his own tomatoes. Didn't want to go to the Farmer's Market. Chad knew in the end that Uncle Dick would get his way so he'd shaken his head and left the two still at it.

Now all the old bad feelings about his father, the violent man he used to be, ballooned up within Chad. He lived here with Uncle Dick, who'd taken him in when he'd gotten out of prison on charges of DUI and assaulting an officer and more. He'd completed his parole and was now a free man. *But everyone will think this is Dad's fault.* The thought clutched Chad's chest and squeezed. No. Over two years of sobriety had changed his father for the good.

One face came to mind. He pulled out his cell. "I'm going to call Tom."

"I wanted to call Shirley," Jessie said. "But she's watching Audra's twins." Chad nodded and tapped Tom's number. Then he thought better of it and cut off the call. Tom was working and had customers. What could he do here? But his heart felt frayed, and Tom would bring comfort. The EMTs kept working, saying words he didn't understand.

Then he thought of the man who could bring real help, a sort of relation to him. And though he didn't want to call him, he tapped his phone and got the local sheriff's voice mail message. He waited, jigging inside, for the beep. "Hey, Carter, Chad Keski here. You're needed at my uncle Dick's place. We called the ambulance for my uncle but it's not just his health. It's not just a medical emergency. He's bruised, bleeding too. Something bad happened here. Come. Please." He disconnected.

Jessie nudged him and they followed the EMTs as they pushed the gurney with Uncle Dick on it toward the ambulance. "You go with your uncle," Jessie urged.

"I just left a message on the sheriff's private line. I got to stay and talk to him." He had to get him here so he could find out the truth before all the ugly rumors about his dad started all over again. Few were ready to believe that Doyle Keski had turned his life around for real.

"You should come with your uncle," one of the EMTs said. "We like to take family with us. It's good for the patient."

Chad was torn.

"I'll stay and wait for the sheriff," Jessie said. "You go. I'll tell Carter everything and then I'll come to the hospital."

Chad let her push him to the ambulance. He loved his great uncle, a gruff but good man. "Okay. But call me...I want to talk to Harding." He always called Sheriff Carter Harding by his last name. Their relationship was unusual, sort of family but sort of not. Chad pushed these idle thoughts away and climbed into the back of the ambulance. Praying for his uncle and his dad. *Dad, what happened? Where are you?*

AS SHE TURNED BACK to the garage, Jessie realized that they hadn't taken care of the fresh fish in their creel. After finding it where Chad had dropped it in the garage, she carried it into the house and paused just inside the hall to the kitchen. This was the remodeled side porch. The old farmhouse had been modified over the years, and the addition of the attached garage had been one change. Next to her was the vintage chest freezer. Should she freeze the fish or just put them into the refrigerator?

It felt foolish thinking of these mundane thoughts when something awful had just happened, but trout were trout. And Dick Blaney loved trout. There was a roll of freezer paper and one of tape on the shelf above the freezer. She tore off what she needed and wrapped each fish individually and then marked them "BT" for brook trout, and the date, and laid them inside the freezer. Being busy with something commonplace for these few moments had distracted her from the feeling of unreality. The day had been perfect and now this. What should she do? Go in? Stay out?

The decision was made for her. A siren sounded coming near, nearer. She walked outside in time to see the county sheriff's car pull up. She waited by the open garage door.

Tall and sturdy, Carter Harding bounded out of his car. "What's happened here?"

Jessie burst into tears. "I don't know," she blubbered. She stopped and took a deep, cleansing breath in through her nose and out through her mouth as her counselor had taught her. Another.

"Start at the beginning," Carter said in a calmer tone.

She did the best she could, trying to keep it short and not give in to tears again. She liked Dick, and seeing violence had triggered memories and sensations she wished she could forget...

Carter had drawn nearer as she spoke. Now he gently gripped her shoulder. "How are you doing?"

Of course he knew why she was crying. Everything that had happened to her over two years ago wanted to rush back, overwhelm her. Forestalling this, she said, "I'm handling it."

He nodded, squeezed her shoulder, and said, "Show me."

She led him through the garage and into the house. "I haven't been farther than here." She told him about the trout and he flashed a brief smile.

"Has anyone else been inside?"

"Chad went in after we called for help. He was worried about his dad...maybe his dad was inside and hurt too."

Carter nodded again, but looked as if he were weighing her words. "You wait here. I'll take a look around."

He motioned toward an old, scarred bench opposite the freezer and she went and sat down on it. She began praying and hoping. How was Dick? She wished she'd been able to go with Chad. He'd looked...devastated.

Lost in the misery she was fighting, she was still aware of Carter's footsteps on the wood floor and going up the stairs to the second floor. Finally, he returned. "Upstairs hasn't been touched, but I think there was a fight of some sort in the living room inside the front door. Looks to me as if someone forced their way in. Do you know where Chad's dad is?"

"No. He should be here. We were going to grill the trout, and he likes to do that."

Carter propped his hands on his belt. "I don't like this."

To Jessie, that sounded like an understatement of some magnitude. She waited for the sheriff to tell her what came next. But he just stared, as if his mind was working.

"Chad wanted to talk to you," she said finally.

"I want to talk to him too. But first I need to get my people going over this crime scene." He pulled out his phone.

"If you don't need me," she said, her desire to be with

Chad and help him prodding her, "I'm going to the hospital. Chad's alone."

"Go. I'll handle this and come there when I can." He turned and began talking into his cell.

Jessie hurried to her little blue car parked in the shade, and soon she was driving south to Ashford and the nearest hospital. And praying for Dick, Chad, and his dad. What had happened while she and Chad fished so near and without a care?

Chapter 2

One leg jittering, Chad sat on the hard ER waiting room chair, barely able to keep himself seated. All the while he wondered why the EMTs had urged him to come with his uncle. The hospital staff wasn't letting him in the area where his uncle was being treated. Well, he couldn't blame them. His uncle had been swarmed with a doctor, nurses, and other techs coming and going. There just hadn't been enough room for him.

Vaguely aware of muted voices around him, Chad tried to pray like Tom, his foster father, had taught him. But all he could manage was a silent chant of "Please, God, please." Maybe that was enough. Breathing in the medicinal scent that said "hospital," he bent his head into his hand and tried to keep calm. Uncle Dick had been breathing. He hadn't been having a heart attack. And the ambulance had got him here in time. All good.

He looked around. Jessie had said she'd come as soon as she could. How long would she have to stay with the sheriff? The worry of what people would say when they heard about this tried to rear up and take him down. He resisted it. Something bad had happened. Yet he knew when his father was sober, he wasn't violent. And he'd been as sober as a preacher when Chad and Jessie had left to go angling. So something totally unexpected and really bad had happened. But what?

"Hey, Chad, what are you doin' here?"

At the sound of the voice, his agitation went into spin cycle. The last person in Winfield County he wanted to see hovered into view. Florence LaVesque, Tom and Shirley's neighbor, a burly older woman who wore her silvered black hair pulled back into a long tail. She always dressed in a mix of hers and her late husband's clothing. And she had a big mouth—always fully loaded—but never with the safety on. He nearly cursed under his breath. But following the manners Tom had drilled into him, Chad rose politely. "Hi, Mrs. LaVesque."

"What are you doin' here?" she repeated. Then she looked shocked. "It ain't Dick, is it? Your uncle?"

Chad nodded, the faint hope she'd leave soon disappearing.

Florence plumped down in the molded plastic chair beside his.

And he sank back onto his, miserable all over, just thinking about what might be happening to his uncle. And what would this "friendly" neighbor say?

"What happened? Another heart attack?" Her voice betrayed a true concern, not just a plea for gossip.

"Not a heart attack." Chad gripped his self-control and spoke as calmly as he could. "Jessie and I went fishing for trout for supper and came home and found him in the garage, unconscious, with his head bleeding."

Florence emitted a sound of shock. "No."

He nodded, his mood sinking lower.

"Is your dad in there with him?" With a nod of her head, she indicated the hall where the emergency patients were being treated.

Her question putting some blame on his dad was exactly what he had been dreading. "No." And that's all he would say.

She looked puzzled and dissatisfied with his response, as if she'd tasted something she was about to spit out.

"How long you been here?" she asked.

He glanced at his watch. "Nearly an hour now."

"You call Shirley? Tom?"

Chad relayed the explanation about why he hadn't contacted them. The Robsons were the couple that had taken him in as a troubled teen and fostered him. He still boarded in their house and so did Jessie. "So I didn't want to worry them. I'll call them when I know what's wrong with Uncle Dick."

She nodded sagely. "Probably best. My ride isn't back, so I'll wait with you. I just came to get a lab done. I don't have to hurry."

He groaned silently and the groan went all the way down to his toes. He might as well call the local radio station and announce the facts now that Florence was here. Was there any way he could urge her to leave? Would that do any good?

Just then the automatic doors opened and Jessie hurried inside. She paused, looking for him he knew.

He rose. "Jess."

She covered the linoleum between them in seconds. "Chad."

They didn't usually touch, but when she gave his arm a quick squeeze, he realized he needed that more than he wanted to admit even to himself. Something inside him eased.

———

JESSIE SIZED up Chad and then noticed Florence, their neighbor, sitting beside him. Her stomach did a jig. Not Florence, always ready to pour salt and sand into a wound. "Florence, what brings you here?" she asked in a polite tone.

Florence nodded toward a hospital wing. "I came here for labs and saw Chad. I have been sittin' with him."

Jessie exchanged a glance with Chad. She knew he wasn't happy. And she couldn't tell him what he was wanting to hear, about the sheriff and what was happening at his uncle's house. But she smiled at the older woman who she actually liked but who even Shirley herself was careful about what she said within her hearing. "Good. Any news?"

Just then a white-coated doctor came through the automatic doors and headed toward them. "Are you Mr. Blaney's nephew?"

Rising with a faint hope, Chad turned to him. "Yes. How is Uncle Dick?"

"He's regained consciousness and we're in the middle of doing tests to see exactly what his injuries are. We're going to keep him overnight. The fact that he was unconscious is concerning. He also has facial contusions and abrasions. Was there some kind of altercation?" The doctor looked at Chad with an appraising look.

Jessie moved closer to Chad, giving him her support.

"An altercation? You mean a fight?" Florence squawked. She turned on Chad. "What's your worthless father done now?"

The doctor looked shocked at her outburst.

Jessie moved forward toward the woman, forestalling Chad from responding. "Florence, Chad's father didn't do this. Please don't jump to baseless conclusions. Something bad happened at Dick's today. The sheriff is there now going over everything."

The doctor didn't look happy about this information.

Florence frowned. "Where's Doyle then?"

"My father wasn't there when we found Uncle Dick," Chad said, sounding grudging. "But the two of them were doing fine when we left them a couple of hours ago."

"Your dad sober?" Florence asked.

"Yes, he was sober," Chad said, his voice trembling with suppressed anger.

"So Mr. Blaney was involved in some kind of physical altercation?" the doctor said, asking for clarification.

"It looked like that," Chad admitted, shoving his hands in his jeans pockets.

Everyone just looked at each other. Jessie thought, *What more is there to say?*

"Hmmm!" Florence shook her head. Then she glanced toward the glass doors. "There's my ride. Gotta go." She looked hard at Chad. "You make sure you let Shirley know how Dick's doing."

Chad nodded, but looked nettled.

Jessie touched his sleeve as they watched the older woman hurry away. The doctor excused himself, saying he'd have someone come for Chad when Mr. Blaney was settled in his room.

Chad and Jessie watched him hurry down the hall and disappear through the inner doors. "We can't help what people say," she murmured.

Chad drew in a long breath. "I know, but about my dad, it's never good."

She squeezed his arm, not wanting to say he was right. She knew what it felt like to be an object of conjecture and gossip. No fun.

Jessie glanced at her watch with a sinking feeling. "I'll have to go soon. I need to get my dough ready to rise overnight in the cooler." After working for Audra in her morning cafe bakeshop for the past two years, she had begun making artisan loaves of bread that sold out every morning to tourists. She was saving for maybe buying a house sometime in the future. And for the lean winter off-season too.

"I know. I'll be up with Uncle Dick soon. Do you think I should ask him about what happened?"

She considered this. "Why don't you play it by ear? Let him lead the conversation…if any. He might be too wiped out to talk or he might not remember. I mean, a possible head injury." She shrugged.

He turned to her and for the first time ever, pulled her close. "That makes sense. Now go. I'll be fine. You can tell Audra what's happened."

During the moments pressed against him, something fluttered alive inside Jessie. She couldn't identify what. Still, she gave him one more hug. "I'll be praying."

He nodded and then released her.

Reluctantly she turned and headed for the door, doing what she'd promised. Praying.

⸺

HEARING HEAVY FOOTSTEPS NEARING, Chad looked toward the room's doorway and saw Harding enter. He'd been waiting for what felt like days for some news, some information. He tamped down his eagerness. The sheriff glanced around the room and toward the window.

Though it was evening now, the summer sun still glowed golden in the narrow window. Uncle Dick had lapsed into an uneasy sleep. The second bed in the room was empty, so thankfully the sheriff and he could talk without being overheard. Chad stood. "Did you find my dad?" he blurted out though he kept his voice low.

Harding shook his head. "I came to see how Dick is doing —if he is able to answer questions—and to discuss a few things we found at Dick's. My deputies are still working the crime scene."

Chad swallowed down his reaction to those final two words. "Okay."

His expression a combination of concern and dismay,

Harding approached the bedside. "I can see that I won't be able to question your uncle until his doctor okays it."

Chad nodded. What else could he do?

"Since your uncle is asleep, why don't we go down to the cafeteria and get a bite. It's about to close, and I haven't had anything since a long-ago lunch."

Chad hated to leave his uncle but he was asleep and Harding's mention of food had triggered Chad's empty stomach to growl. "Okay. But I'm staying the night."

Harding nodded and, neither talking, they went down the elevator to the basement cafeteria, which was nearly empty. The cafeteria food line also proved nearly depleted. Both of them made do with ham and cheese subs, chips, and tall glasses of pop. The kitchen crew was already cleaning up, soon to close.

After they sat down at a table near the door, Harding asked, "What did the doctor say about Dick's condition?"

Chad hated to put this into words but he replied with the doctor's final assessment, "A couple of cracked ribs, facial contusions and lacerations, and a mild concussion."

"Is he going to be all right?"

Chad sincerely hoped so. The sick feeling he'd carried inside ever since seeing his uncle lying on the garage floor would not lift. But his stomach growled and he picked up his sandwich. "The doctor said he needs watching because of the concussion but fortunately…whatever happened didn't trigger another heart attack." His voice caught on the last two words.

"I'm glad."

"Me too." Chad finally bit into his sandwich. It would be a long time till breakfast.

Harding chewed another bite of sandwich and then said, "We aren't finished with the crime scene."

Chad didn't know if he should ask what they found at Uncle Dick's or not. *But I want to know, need to know.*

"We didn't," Harding continued, "find a lot, but we have some evidence that will be sent to the state crime lab ASAP."

Chad wondered what they had found. He'd only seen a torn-up living room and Uncle Dick bleeding.

"Your initial assessment that there had been a fight in your uncle's living room appears to be accurate. We're searching not only the house but also the grounds. I put out an APB on your dad's truck."

Chad contrasted Harding's voice now to the way he usually sounded at home or at Tom's house. This sounded official. "Okay…"

"What we found is troubling."

Chad waited, his sandwich held in midair.

"We found your father's phone outside, smashed and tossed into the grass."

Chad drew in a breath.

"Also Dick's wallet, emptied and discarded in the bushes outside the front door." The sheriff paused. "We were able to get some prints from that. But we'll need to get Dick's prints to rule them out."

Chad waited for the worst to come.

"We also found a little blood splatter on the wall near the front door, probably from a fight, not a gunshot."

Chad put down his sandwich. "Whose blood? How much?"

"Not as much as if it had been the result of a gunshot, but commensurate with a fistfight. It will be sent to the state lab for DNA testing. The process will take longer to get results than it does on TV." His mouth twisted wryly.

Was the sheriff thinking that his father had been hurt too? An unexpected darkness opened inside Chad.

"You know that every felon's DNA is kept on file?"

Chad nodded at this information.

Harding set down his sandwich too. "This is what I think happened. Since your father and his uncle have been living together for over two years and getting along, I think someone entered the house, was challenged, and a fight took place. I don't know where your father is now. We couldn't find any clue to a second vehicle except for some tire tracks. Your father's truck is missing, so he might have pursued the intruders, but I would have expected him to call for backup."

"Maybe, because they smashed his phone, he couldn't call," Chad interjected.

"Yes, but he might yet find a public pay phone and call when he can."

Chad looked down at the sandwich he knew he should eat but that had lost its appeal.

"Or there was more than one intruder and they stole the truck and took your dad with them." Harding paused to sip his drink and probably to give Chad time to take this in.

Chad shook his head, trying to clear it. After he'd been removed from his father's custody in his early teens, he'd kept as far from him and his destructive life as possible. "Why would they want my dad? He lives on pay from odd jobs. I can't figure out what happened." Unable to stop himself, he added, "But you know everyone will blame this on my dad."

Harding nodded. "I'm afraid that's true, but I'm keeping an open mind. All I know for sure is that something violent happened at your uncle's today. I intend to find out what. And locate your father."

Chad drew in his first easy or easier breath since arriving at his uncle's house hours ago. He knew from experience he could trust Harding to keep his word. Still, worry sat in his stomach like a big lump of rough granite. How would this all end? Was worse coming?

Chapter 3

Late July 10th

Voices… Pain… A motor rumbling. Bones rattling. Doyle felt himself groan, but didn't hear it. He forced his eyes open. Blinking, he tried to focus and couldn't. Where? He tried to draw a deep breath and gagged against the twisted cloth tied in his mouth and around his head. He tried to reach up and pull it off, but his hands were bound behind him. Pain. He gasped for breath. He moved his feet and found his ankles bound tightly together.

What had happened? He tried to think. Then images flashed in his mind. They'd come. Forced their way in. Remembered fear leaped inside him like a wolf ripping apart its kill. His heart pounded. *They must have taken me with them. But why?*

Uncle Dick! He closed his eyes but he couldn't shut out the image of his uncle ordering them out of his house. And then they'd attacked his uncle. *I tried,* Doyle thought, *I tried to protect him.* Tears wet his eyes. Had they killed Uncle Dick?

It didn't make sense. Why had they broken in? Uncle Dick didn't have anything anyone would want. Who were they?

Something triggered in his mind. It was just out of his reach. Did he know them? Why couldn't he remember? He tried to pray like he'd heard his son pray but all he could come up with was, *God, Dick Blaney is a good man. Don't let him die. Don't let him be dead.*

━━━

JULY 11TH

Chad did not want to leave the hospital, leave his sleeping uncle Dick. But he had a job. July was the heart of the busy tourist season. Audra counted on him to get to her place and start the sweet roll dough well before dawn. People lined up every morning for her coffee, teas, and great bakery treats. So he left the sleeping hospital via the Emergency exit, his footsteps loud to his ears. He wished he could stop at home, take a shower and change; however, the clock made the decision for him. Yeast dough needed time to rise.

In the cool morning gray, he drove to Audra's Victorian that stood three stories high across from the wharf. He parked in the alley lined with dandelions and wild grass and let himself into the rear kitchen entrance. He locked the door behind him and glanced around at the stainless steel and white commercial kitchen. Neatly arranged around a large island were refrigerators, freezers, and ovens, even a pizza oven. He began his day as usual by washing his hands. He felt funny to be here dressed in his fishing outfit, the shirt with all those pockets.

Yet being in this familiar place again began to relax him. If only the memories of yesterday, of finding Uncle Dick bleeding, didn't leave him wondering and uncertain. He dried his hands, put on his crisp white baker's apron, and threw himself into his work. After the routine of weighing or measuring the ingredients into the large mixer with the dough hook, he watched the dough swirl in the bowl.

A sudden weakness swamped him. He didn't like not knowing what to do, how to help his uncle, his father. He leaned forward, bracing himself with his palms against the edge of the stainless steel counter. He sent the same prayer he'd repeated all night heavenward. *Heal Uncle Dick and protect my dad wherever he is, please.* His mind tried to take him down the path of thinking his father might already be lying dead somewhere.

If that was true, then all the progress they'd accomplished learning how to forgive and learning how to be father and son would be for nothing. He forced his mind away from that possibility. Many times in the past, before Shirley had taken him in, he'd wished his father to disappear. Now his dad had disappeared and Chad felt only guilt and loss.

"I still can't figure out what happened," he said to the empty room. He spoke softly because Audra and her family were sleeping over his head on the second floor of the old house that she and Harding had renovated. He turned to prepping the nuts and raisins and blending the various seasoning mixtures that would flavor the different sweet rolls he'd form from the dough after its first proving.

Then he allowed himself to make the first pot of coffee for the day. He stepped outside with his mug. Breathing in the combination of fresh air and fragrant coffee, he sat down on the bench by the door and leaned back to watch the sun rise. From the faint glow on the horizon behind the houses and the rising forest behind them, the sun rose, radiant in the pink sky. Yet awful possibilities kept trying to take over his mind and make his heart race. As he watched the pink dawn progress to a blue sky, he fought the darkness from these thoughts with the same prayer. *God take care of Uncle Dick and my dad. Please.*

Finally, after checking his watch, he got up and went inside to get his vat of dough out of the proving drawer and begin to shape it into sweet rolls for the next rise.

What he saw stopped him. He stared at the dough, dumbfounded. "Why didn't you rise?"

He glanced around to the counter where his ingredients still sat. When he realized what he'd done, anger surged through him like a runaway train. He cursed aloud.

The door behind him opened.

Disgusted, he picked up the bowl of unrisen dough and turned to throw it outside.

"Chad!" Jessie's voice stopped him.

He stood there, holding onto the rim of the stainless steel bowl, heaving with unexpected rage.

"I came early so I could help you," she explained as she hung her purse on a peg. "What's wrong?"

"I forgot to add the yeast," he said in a gritty voice, still clogged with disgust at himself.

"Well, that happens. What can we do with the dough then?"

Chad just stared at her.

"How about those breadsticks we tried earlier this spring? I'll just roll it out, slice it into strips, brush them with an egg wash, and sprinkle a lot of cinnamon sugar on them. They'll sell."

Chad drew in a deep breath. He worked at tamping down his anger. "Okay, but I don't have time to do that and get another batch—"

"I came early so I could help you," she repeated. "Use the fast-acting yeast this time. I'll check the rise on my loaves and then I'll do the cinnamon sticks." She walked over and lifted the bowl from his hands.

Chad watched Jess begin doing work she didn't have to. He was ashamed of himself. Tom never lost his temper and cursed. He stared at the gray slate tile floor.

Then he felt Jess touch his shoulder. "You're going through a bad time. You know I lost my temper when I..." Her voice trailed off. They never talked about the early spring two years ago when she'd turned up here, lying unconscious in the snow.

He looked into her face, one so familiar to him...so pretty. Shocked at this unexpected thought, he swallowed, trying to moisten his mouth to be able to answer her.

"I can't tell you everything will all work out, but I can tell you that you're not alone." She squeezed his upper arm.

Before she could move away, he pressed his hand over hers. "Thanks, Jess." His voice still sounded gravelly, and he felt tired, as if he'd sprinted a few blocks. He kept his hand over her smaller soft one, wanting, needing this connection with her. He stared into her eyes, really studied them for the first time. They weren't as dark as his. Somehow gold flecks ringed her irises. It was like she had gold dust in her eyes. He couldn't look away.

She squeezed his arm again, then pulled away, peeking at her bread dough in the large refrigerator and then turning to his unleavened dough. She dumped it out of the bowl and began rolling it out.

He stood for a moment just watching her. He'd been with Jess on and off practically every day over the past two years since she moved into Shirley's and lived in the attic above the room he rented there. Why had he never before noticed how unusual her eyes were? How attractive? He swallowed down something he couldn't identify and turned again to mix more sweet dough. And hoped it would be ready when Audra entered the kitchen...soon.

THE BREADSTICKS HAD SOLD out in just over an hour and Audra had laughed when he told her about leaving out the yeast. She pronounced it Serendipity. Chad had seen the usual kindness in Audra's eyes.

So his day had followed its usual tourist season routine. After working at the bakery in the morning, he now had a few free hours before he'd be expected to help Tom at the garage. He'd taken advantage of this opening. Concern for Uncle Dick had spurred him to drive to Ashford. He arrived in the hall outside his uncle's hospital room only to hear Harding's voice. Evidently he'd just gotten there too. Chad remembered that Harding had told him last night that he needed to question Uncle Dick as soon as it was possible. Was Uncle Dick already well enough to talk about what had happened? That was good, right?

Then Chad heard another voice. It sounded like a doctor. "Mr. Blaney has sustained a concussion, so I'm concerned, Sheriff, that you don't press him too hard—"

"I'm fine. I got a hard head." Uncle Dick's irritated voice cut the doctor off.

Chad grinned. Hearing his uncle's customary curmudgeonly voice lifted some deep part of him. Uncle Dick was family. Good family. Chad leaned back against the wall, ready to eavesdrop without guilt.

"Dick, you know what I need to hear," Harding said.

"You want to know what happened at my place yesterday."

"Yes."

"Where's Doyle?" Uncle Dick asked.

Chad felt his gut tighten. Subdued voices sounded from down the hall. He glanced but he couldn't see anyone.

"We don't know Doyle's whereabouts." Harding sounded apologetic.

Dick grunted. "He hasn't turned up? That's bad. These guys were trouble, all right. Busted through my front door and started pushing Doyle around. I told them to get out and—"

"How many were there?" Harding asked.

A pause. "Three. We were outnumbered from the get-go."

"Can you give me any descriptions?"

"Two of them looked like they'd spent a lot of time at a gym. Muscles. They call them big guns now, you know. The third was a long drink of water, but he gave the orders."

"Any details? Anything that stood out?"

"They all have some kind of a tattoo—like they were done by somebody who didn't know what he was doing."

Chad had seen something like this on his dad. Prison tats?

"One guy was bald. None of them were dressed what you'd call well. Scruffy like."

"They began a fight?" Harding prompted.

"Yeah, but Doyle and me weren't up to it. They knocked him out pretty fast. Then chased me. I was trying to get to the kitchen phone to call 911, but they chased me into the garage. That's all I can remember about what happened. It was fast, you know? Last night Chad told me his dad wasn't there when he and that sweet Jessie girl got back from fishin'."

Chad frowned. He hadn't wanted to tell Uncle Dick that, but his great uncle had pressed him so he'd told him just the least he could.

Harding cleared his throat. A phone rang somewhere down the floor. "That's right. We don't know if he pursued them or if they took him and his truck. I can't seem to get a bead on what this is besides the obvious, a home invasion and assault on you and now, it seems, on Doyle. And maybe a kidnapping."

"They were a nasty bunch. I wish I could remember more." Uncle Dick sounded uncharacteristically uncertain.

"Anything else?"

"Not now. I'm still beat. A nasty bunch," Uncle Dick repeated. "That's all I got for you, Sheriff. I wish I'd used my head and run for the phone right off instead of... But I'm used to taking care of myself."

"I'm the same—" Harding began.

"Hey, what you doin' out here?" Florence's voice snapped Chad's head around. "Is there some reason you're hanging around in the hall? Is something goin' on with Dick? Is he bad?"

Chad gritted his teeth, holding back sharp words.

Now aware of their presence, Harding summoned them both, "Come on in, Florence. Is Chad with you?"

"Yes, I'm out here. I didn't want to interrupt you," Chad said, trying not to sound as irritated as he felt. He followed Florence into the room.

Harding rose from the chair by the bed. "Florence, I heard you were here yesterday when Dick was brought in."

"Flo," Dick said in gruff greeting. "You come to hassle me?"

"Me? You're the one who's always saying something to stir everybody up."

Chad lingered by the door.

"Chad," his uncle greeted him. "You off work?"

"In between jobs like usual. Just wanted to check on you." *I was worried.*

Uncle Dick addressed the words he hadn't spoken. "I'm going to be okay. Doc says I'll probably be goin' home tomorrow. Come in."

Chad replied from the doorway, "No. Just wanted to see you. I got to get to Tom's. You got company." He nodded toward Florence.

"They'll find your dad, son," Uncle Dick said, sounding or trying to sound reassuring. "It's just going to take time."

Chad nodded out of politeness. "I'll be back later."

Uncle Dick turned to his other visitor. "You bring a deck of cards with you, Flo?"

A nurse walked in, looked at the monitor, and took notes.

Harding waved Florence to the chair. "I'll be in touch, Dick."

Before Chad could get away, he overheard Florence say just what he'd expected her to say. "I told you not to take in that good-for-nothing nephew of yours. Now what has he brought down on you?"

Uncle Dick retorted, "Doyle's not to blame—"

Harding motioned Chad to follow him down the hall and out of the hospital. Chad was glad to leave. Outside in the July warmth, he admitted, "I heard what Uncle Dick told you."

"Not much."

"No." Chad looked around the parking lot. "What about the blood sample you took?" He hoped Harding would tell him if he knew anything.

"I've already sent the samples to the state lab for DNA testing. Let's hope they match some sample on file."

Chad chewed on this, not knowing if it would turn out good or not.

Harding studied him. "The investigation has just started, Chad. Dick looks like he'll be all right, and we'll find your dad. Have some faith."

Chad nodded but only once as if his neck had stiffened. He had some faith, but did he have enough?

Harding's phone rang and he began talking into it as he walked away.

Chad caught the words, "That's promising. I'll get right over there."

What was promising? Chad nearly started to follow the sheriff, but then he stopped. If Harding wanted him, he'd let him know.

He didn't.

Chad got into his pickup and started for home. He would stop and eat lunch before Tom needed him at the garage. Again Chad started praying, something he'd done more of over the past twenty-four hours than ever before.

Chapter 4

July 11th

Under the golden sun and well after lunch, Jessie had just finished up cleaning out Nick Reynold's dog yard. Nick raced his team of Alaskan huskies in various sled dog races. The sport was his passion. Usually his wife, Megan, the daughter of the woman who'd helped Jessie so much when she landed in Winfield, usually helped him with dog care. But Megan was early in her pregnancy, and the heat enhanced the scent of "dog-do." So Jessie had offered to help out. Of course, they insisted on paying her, but she refused to take more than minimum wage. She owed Megan's mom, Lois, so much more than could ever be repaid in money.

Out of the corner of her eye, she glimpsed the sheriff's silver-blue SUV drive up the tree-lined lane to the two-story log home. Tall, dark Nick, who had uncharacteristically left her to do all the work alone, hurried outside and began an intense conversation with Carter Harding, his brother-in-law. The two had married sisters, Audra and Megan.

Wondering what had prompted this visit, Jessie petted the last blue-eyed husky and left the yard. A few of the chained huskies yodeled at her in farewell. Maddie, Nick's husky that was a house pet, followed Jessie as she stowed the shovel and work gloves in the nearby shed. She turned to watch the sheriff and Nick hurry into the house. She could not help but suspect that this had something to do with what had happened at Dick's. Nick was Dick's closest neighbor though you couldn't see one house from the other through the thick forest that dominated each property.

Before she left, she always stopped in to chat with Megan. And this time she wanted, needed to find out what was going on. She would eavesdrop, if possible, or ask outright, if necessary. Chad should be privy to what was going on. Her mind filled with the image of Chad's downcast face this morning at work at Audra's as he'd threatened to dump the vat of unrisen, "spoiled" dough. She walked to the screen door, politely knocked on its wooden frame, and was called in.

Megan stood at the sink, washing ruffled leaves.

"What are you making?" Jessie asked, her ears straining to sort out the voices in the den. The great room she had entered, decorated with wood and outdoorsy furniture with a rustic fireplace, combined the living room, dining room, and kitchen areas.

"Just got a delivery of greens from that local farmer we contracted with. Making a big salad for supper."

"Sounds good." Jessie couldn't stop herself from asking, "What's the sheriff doing here?"

Megan turned away from the sink, toward Jessie and the half-opened door to Nick's den. "I think Nick found something on one of those motion-activated cameras he put up the first year he moved north year-round. He did it before he raced that first year in February."

Jessie had been told the story of how Megan and Nick met here and all the bad things that had endangered his dogs that year, the year he'd been preparing for his first formal sled dog race. "I didn't know he still had any cameras up."

"He still keeps a couple around the property. I kid him about it, but you know how he is with his team. He doesn't want anything bad or dangerous to happen to them."

Jessie, more focused on the den, replied politely, "I hear you. I love those dogs too. So sweet and eager to please."

The men came out of the room and halted when they saw the women looking at them.

"That's right, Jessie," the sheriff said as if remembering why she was here. "I heard you were helping out with Nick's dogs."

Jessie nodded, curiosity riddling her. "So what's up?" She tried to keep her voice casual.

The four of them paused, looking at each other.

"So?" Megan challenged them in her usual style. "What's going on?"

The two men exchanged glances. "We may have a lead," the sheriff said. "It might not pay out, but at least it's something to follow up on."

Okay, Jessie replied silently, and…

"Thanks for contacting me, Nick." The sheriff shook Nick's hand and was out the door.

Since the sheriff had withheld any details, Jessie and Megan gazed expectantly at Nick.

Nick gave in. "You remember the strong winds we had earlier this week?"

"Yesss…" Megan replied, prompting more.

"Well, it whipped one of the cameras at the entrance to our lane around toward Blaney's. I got some footage I thought Carter would want to see. He's taking it in to find out if he can enhance the images and get more info."

"What's on the footage?" Megan asked.

Jessie was glad she was taking the lead in this.

31

Nick frowned. "Just some footage of vehicles on the county highway that goes by our drive and the start of Blaney's lane."

Jessie considered this. "You mean you might have filmed some vehicles going into Dick's lane?"

"Yes, and coming out. But Carter didn't know if it would be any help or not. Those cameras aren't very high resolution —really fuzzy." He shrugged. "It might help his investigation or it might be a bust."

"Okay," Jessie conceded with the best grace she could manage. "Do you need me for anything else now?"

"No, thanks so much," Megan answered for them. "I hope this queasiness will go away soon. I thought morning sickness was just for the mornings, but I have it all day." She scrunched up her face.

Grinning wryly, Jessie patted her arm. "It's all worth it."

"That's what everybody keeps telling me, but they're not the ones feeling queasy!"

Jessie chuckled and turned to leave. She was supposed to help Shirley with laundry today. Her days were busy and she liked that, but this new information posed a conundrum for her. Should she call Chad or wait till she had more information?

As she climbed into her little blue car, she decided to wait a bit. Chad needed encouragement, but she didn't want to get his hopes up. This possible lead might go nowhere. If the video actually helped, the sheriff would tell him. After all, Chad and Carter were almost family. And if this proved a dead end, she didn't want to spark more discouragement. *Oh, dear Lord, help.*

⸻

STRETCHING HIS BACK MUSCLES, Chad had just finished another oil change at Tom's Garage, a block from Audra's. The late afternoon sun slanted in through the open bay door.

This morning he had worn his fishing outfit under a white apron at Audra's, then he'd showered and gone to put on his jeans and T-shirt to visit Uncle Dick. Now he wore his garage work clothes. So many changes in one day.

Nearby Tom was busy on another car, his head under the older Jeep's dark hood. He was muttering to himself and clanging metal on metal occasionally as he worked.

Chad knew that a lot of seasonal people actually saved their regular maintenance till they came north. They liked Tom and wanted him to look over their cars and tell them exactly what needed to be done. Even though he was a small-town garage owner, Tom kept up with the latest manuals and had all the equipment he needed to stay current in auto repair. His shop, occupying a 1930s cement-block gas station, looked like a vintage auto shop, but it was very much in the twenty-first century.

Thirsty and needing a break, Chad headed over to the pop machine. Gasoline, grease, and oil scented the air.

As usual, the shop radio was tuned to the Ashford station that featured local news over national events and played a variety of golden oldies from the '50s through the '80s. Now a 1960s song, something about a Paul and Paula who evidently were an "item," was ending.

Just as he reached into his pocket, pulling out change, the local interview show done by Vance Sheridan began. In his low conversational voice, Vance said, "The guest I had intended to interview wasn't able to keep his appointment with me. But fortunately, just moments ago, I received a call from Sheriff Harding, asking for our help. He's at his office on the phone. Hello, Sheriff, what is the help you need from our local residents and visitors?"

Chad halted in the process of inserting coins into the machine. What had Harding discovered? He turned toward the radio as if that would help him hear better. His arm dropped to his side.

"Thanks, Sheridan. I'm sure everyone has heard about yesterday's attack on Dick Blaney. Some new evidence in connection with that home invasion has come to light, and I need everyone to think back to yesterday late in the afternoon."

Unable to move, Chad gripped the quarters in his hand. They dug into his palm.

Sheridan murmured, "Fortunately we don't get many incidents like that here in the northwoods. I'm sure our people will want to help in any way they can."

From the corner of his eye, Chad saw movement. A wrench in hand, Tom drew out from under the hood and looked to him. Chad glanced at him and then looked down.

The sheriff went on. "We've already been trying to get a line on the vehicle that the attackers must have used to get to the scene of the crime. But earlier today a local resident contacted me. He had some brief video footage of two vehicles near Blaney's at the time in question. The video shows a vehicle I know well, an older truck belonging to Doyle Keski, and another vehicle that may lead us to who did this. As I said, the footage is brief, actually just two clips, and really grainy. We worked with it and were able to get some better resolution, but it's still unclear. We don't think the driver of the Keski vehicle is Doyle, but we can't be certain. It's that blurry."

Hearing his dad's name mentioned, Chad could hardly draw breath.

He heard Tom moving his way.

"So what exactly do you need?" Sheridan asked.

"I'm going to give the description of both vehicles. One drove in alone, and then after a few minutes drove out with the Keski truck following it and heading south. We couldn't get a clear look at the license plate. But here's the description of the unknown vehicle: a dark older sedan with a dented front passenger door.

"We are asking everyone who was on County Highway J on that day to think of the vehicles they might have seen heading south. I'll give your listeners the number to call if they think they have any helpful information. Anything." The sheriff gave the number slowly twice. "Any and all information will be appreciated. Our hope is that with citizen cooperation we may find a lead to who attacked Dick Blaney."

Tom had reached Chad and rested a hand on his shoulder. "I wish Carter had called here first."

Chad nodded, feeling rooted to the concrete floor and sucked dry.

"But I would bet that he didn't have a choice about the timing of the broadcast. The host needed Carter on short notice since his scheduled guest bailed."

Chad nodded again, feeling like a wind-up toy.

Tom took the coins from his hand and inserted them for him, and they clicked one by one. He selected Chad's favorite pop and handed him the cold can after it was dispensed. "Carter did say that it looked like your father's truck was not driven by him. That's good news in one way and bad in another."

Chad drew in a breath, then opened his pop can and drank deeply of the sweet, bubbly liquid. It contrasted with the solid brick of ice in his stomach. He considered Tom's words about his dad. "Yeah, maybe, but that won't stop the gossip."

Tom squeezed his shoulder. "I'm praying for your dad. I don't think he'd do anything to harm Dick. He's really changed so much and is so grateful to Dick. I know it hurts when people think bad things, but it's the truth that's important. 'The truth will out,' Shakespeare wrote. And he's still right. Keep faith, son."

Too choked up to reply, Chad turned to Tom. Only the two

of them were in the shop. He wrapped his arms around Tom, one of the few spontaneous hugs he'd ever given him. Tom returned the hug. Once again Chad was thankful for this good man. When Tom married Shirley, he became Chad's foster father. *I'm so blessed.*

Chad's phone rang, and he drew away to pull it from his pocket. "Jess?"

"Chad, I know you'll be done at Tom's soon. I think after supper at Shirley's, we should go over to Dick's to clean his place before he comes home tomorrow. Why don't you call the sheriff's office and see if it's okay?"

Chad, grabbing at the excuse to contact Harding, consented.

"Call me. I want to go with you."

"Okay." After ending Jess's call, he tapped Harding's number. Leave it to Jess to think of this. Had she heard the sheriff on the radio too?

━━

RIDING IN CHAD'S TRUCK, Jessie watched the scenery go by, the summer green leaves, true-blue sky, and white puffy clouds, so beautiful. No wonder people came from all over to spend even a weekend here in the forest on the shore of Lake Superior. The sun rode lower in the sky, a summer twilight. She hoped what she planned to suggest to Chad was the right thing.

Chad turned into Dick's lane and Jessie's stomach cinched as the memories of what had happened to her and what she'd seen just yesterday flowed through her mind.

"Jess, I'm glad you thought of us coming to clean up Uncle Dick's place before he comes home tomorrow." Chad didn't sound like himself.

And that tugged at her heart. He was such a good guy and

tried so hard to live down his father's bad rep. Of course, she wouldn't say any of that, but she wanted in the worst or really the best way to help him in this awful time. But how? She suppressed the urge to touch his arm. "I'm glad I called Carter and he said they're done with it as a crime scene. And I want it to be…"

"Back to normal," Chad finished for her.

"Right." Jess felt the reassurance she always did. Chad understood her, better even than her parents.

Chad parked in front of the house and they met on the two steps up to the front door. Chad unlocked it with the key Uncle Dick had given him a few years ago. They stepped inside, Jessie first. The disorder in the usually neat living room shocked her. It looked like a war had happened here. A chair was knocked on its side. Lamps had been broken. She drew in a sharp breath. The scene triggered memories from her own past, memories of outbursts of violence. They saturated her and she fought the tide. Chad needed her strong and positive. "Well," she said, concealing her inner turmoil, "now I'm doubly glad we came. Where should we start?"

Chad heaved a long and labored sigh. "First I guess we should put things back upright and weed out the broken stuff. And then I'll get out the vacuum."

"Makes sense. I'll dust." Jessie bent down and picked up a broken lamp. It was vintage '70s but now it was toast, its larger pieces strung together by the electrical cord. "Do you know where he keeps the garbage bags?"

Chad nodded and headed to the kitchen just around the corner toward the rear. Soon the two of them had filled almost two kitchen bags with trashed items. Then Chad got out the vacuum and began working the carpet while she found dust-cloths and began using them on what must have been finger-printing dust. The gray film covered every, and she meant every, surface in the living room and large eat-in kitchen. She tried to think of a diplomatic way to bring up the sheriff's radio interview that she'd heard while sitting at the table in Shirley's kitchen. She had a suggestion for Chad, but how would he take it?

Finally, the vacuum fell silent. *Now or never*, she thought. "Chad, how are you handling all this?" She hurried on. "I know you're upset. Do you want to talk about it? I mean the radio interview?"

He tucked the vacuum back into the front closet where it belonged and turned to her. "I don't...and I do. If my dad wasn't driving the truck, that could mean he didn't go willingly and he might be hurt somewhere."

Jessie heard him quaver on the final two words. Her mind supplied, *Or dead.* She moved to stand in front of him.

"I don't know what to think except that I can't see my dad hurting his uncle. The gist of what Uncle Dick told me and the sheriff is that three guys came in and started the fighting here."

She watched his gaze roam around at the room they'd just worked on and that still needed a lot more cleaning before Dick saw it.

Seeing his bleak expression, Jessie moved closer and put an arm around his shoulders. The time had come to offer her suggestion. "I think you should talk to Carter. I mean just the two of you, away from where he works. You're almost family, and he isn't jumping to any conclusions about your dad. Why don't you call him and ask if you can talk, just the two of you." She emphasized the final phrase.

"What good would that do?" he asked.

"It can't hurt, and it might help you understand what he's doing. That would make you feel less hopeless. I mean, two years ago when I was the big news here, I felt better whenever the sheriff came over to Lois's house and told me some lead he was pursuing. I didn't feel so helpless then."

He moved forward and rested his cheek against hers. "I do feel helpless," he muttered.

"I understand," she whispered. "But talk to Carter. He's a good man, like Tom."

Chad nodded against her cheek.

The contact caused a flutter inside her, one she'd never felt before with Chad. It made her want to step away because the old fear tried to pop up. She resisted it and prolonged the contact for a few more moments. Chad needed her comfort. Then she sighed and took a step toward the kitchen. "We have more work to do. We need to straighten the garage. And wash away the…blood on the floor in there."

"Right. And then we'll take a look at the bedrooms upstairs. I don't think the men went up there but…"

"But the police probably dusted everything there too. Every room will need cleaning," she agreed.

The two of them headed through the kitchen to the garage.

"Will you call Carter?" she asked, looking toward him as she pressed the garage door button.

"Yeah, I will later when we get home. Thanks, Jess. You're a true friend."

She smiled at him over her shoulder, wishing she could do more. The worry on his face was hard to bear. The pull to press her cheek against his reared up. Instead she stepped into the garage. She ignored another unusual prompting to turn and wrap her arms around him. By unspoken agreement, they were friends, best friends, yes, but just friends. And though she wanted that to continue, the pull toward him didn't let up.

Chapter 5

July 12th

Chad had been somewhat surprised when Harding had agreed to meet him at the state park near Winfield. But Harding hadn't asked why. Just agreed to meet him. So after his morning shift at Audra's bakery and coffee shop, Chad sat on top of a picnic table in the clearing near a parking lot, watching for the sheriff's silver and blue SUV. Since it was midweek, the park was nearly deserted. The towering pines surrounded the clearing and the head of a hiking trail stood off to the left of the picnic area.

After arriving here, Chad had asked himself again if this was a good idea. But Jess had insisted he talk to Harding. The image of her talking him down yesterday morning when he nearly tossed out that dough caught him around his heart. *Jess.* He wished she'd come with him, but she was still working with Audra and this was his job to do. He shouldn't worry about this meeting. Since Tom was Harding's stepdad and Chad's foster father, he could count on Harding at least being polite. *So it can't hurt,* he reassured himself, but his gut still stirred, making him feel a bit queasy. He didn't want to face his father's drinking problem, something that had come up time after time. But he wouldn't have long to talk with Harding anyway. He was due to go to the hospital to drive his uncle home sometime after lunch.

The SUV he was waiting for cruised out of the trees into sight. Relief and anxiety enacted a tug of war in his gut. He pushed those down and stood. Harding got out and headed toward him with a cloth over his arm, a large white bag in one hand and a drink carrier in the other.

"I brought lunch," the sheriff announced. "A&W."

Chad had no appetite but he smiled politely.

Harding dropped a large threadbare bath towel down onto the redwood-painted picnic table like a small tablecloth. "I keep this in the car for various reasons. It's clean." He doled out cheeseburgers and fries and lifted the two tall root beers from the carrier. Then he bowed his head, obviously giving thanks.

Chad followed suit.

After a moment they looked at each other across the table, the quiet enfolding them, making Chad tongue-tied. "Eat up," Harding said.

Chad unwrapped his burger. "You knew what I wanted on it," he said with surprise.

Harding chuckled. "I've eaten enough burgers at Shirley's with you. So yeah, catsup, pickles, no onion, no mustard."

Chad felt himself smile. Harding had noticed. Somehow that meant a lot. *But it's just how I like my cheeseburgers, nothing big.* Still, he let this bolster his confidence.

"So, Chad, what did you want to talk to me about?"

The question caught Chad with his mouth full. He held up a hand, finished chewing his first bite, and then swallowed. "I know you're the sheriff and there are things you can't tell me," he began.

"That's right. I don't think you'd go around gossiping, but I don't want to jeopardize the future court case in any way. So I have to be cautious."

Chad nodded and ate a crispy fry. He didn't know how to ask what he really wanted to know. How could he or someone help find his dad?

Harding set his burger down on the mustard-smeared wrapper. "I do have something I know about the case I can share with you. I'm going to be guesting on Sheridan's show again this afternoon and making it public knowledge. He told me to call him if I needed to get any new word out about any lead in this case. People are very upset about what happened to your great uncle."

Chad noticed he said people were concerned about his uncle, but what about his dad? "What is it?" The breeze ruffled the leaves overhead, a soft rustling sound, so opposite to what Chad was feeling.

"Even before getting the video clips from Nick and calling the radio show, I had officers stopping people who were driving in the vicinity of Dick's place about the same time as the incident took place the day before. People often drive the same road at the same time every day. Jobs or family responsibilities, etcetera. A few had seen the dark sedan with your dad's truck."

"Really?" Chad tried to keep his voice level, not reveal the spurt of anxiety within.

"Yes, one of them described the man driving your dad's truck. Said the window was open and the driver was a big guy who had a red beard. A second, unrelated witness mentioned the red-bearded driver too, so that leads me to believe the observation could be valid. Also, they gave the information before the radio interview."

Now Chad knew Jess was right. Just hearing that some progress had been made let him swallow his next bite. But then reality set in. Just validating the video clips and getting a description of the man driving his dad's truck—what could the sheriff do with that? It seemed undeniable now that the attackers had taken his dad with them. He stared down at his fries, wishing his appetite hadn't died.

"There is one thing that could help me. Other than your uncle Dick, did your dad have any friends left around here?"

This question and simultaneously the sound of a bird singing out its name, "Killdeer! Killdeer!" startled Chad. He gazed at Harding, stumped for a reply. Finally he said, "He broke with all his old friends. I mean, if you don't drink anymore, hanging around bars with guys who do…" He lifted his shoulders, not knowing how to finish the sentence.

"Well, if you think of any, we could question them. Okay?"

Chad nodded. The sheriff turned his gaze onto Chad in a way that put him on alert. What was coming now?

"Chad, I've been wanting to talk to you about something else for a while. I mean before all this happened."

Sudden dread weighed on Chad. "What?"

"You're at the age where you need to start thinking of a career—"

The totally unexpected topic took Chad by surprise. "I'm working two jobs—"

"A career is not just two part-time jobs." Harding held up a hand. "Hear me out."

Chad owed this man because of their connection and the fact that he'd come today to talk. He nodded.

"I think you should look into the law enforcement two-year program at the community college south of here."

These words were so unexpected that Chad felt his jaw loosen. "Me?" *A cop?*

"Yes, you." Harding took another bite of his burger.

Chad stared at him. "You're kidding, right?"

Harding frowned. "Why would I do that? I'm serious. I know that you wrongfully carry your dad's bad reputation around on your back. But that's your dad, not you."

Chad snorted. "Tell that to everyone else."

Harding gazed at him. "You know that when I was young, I had a bad rep here. I was wild to a fault. Do you know what I was guilty of in my teens?"

Chad shook his head. But he'd heard that the sheriff had been wild and had had to prove that he'd changed.

"I was at a party where a kid almost died and I was the one in the fight with him. I was seventeen, almost an adult. If the judge had decided to try me as an adult, I would have gone to prison. Instead Tom hired a lawyer and that day changed my life."

Chad noticed how Harding's voice had gotten rough with emotion. "Wow. I didn't know."

"It's not something I talk about, but Tom changed my life that day, changed my direction. I can never thank him enough."

"And he wasn't even your real dad." A doe and her fawn strolled out of the trees on the other side of the parking lot behind Harding. Chad tried to imagine the sheriff as a kid in court. He couldn't.

"That's right, just my stepdad. So if I can become a sheriff, why can't you study law enforcement and become an officer?"

Chad stared at Harding.

"Do you like working with food? Or working with cars?" Harding asked. "Enough to learn more?"

Chad took another bite of burger, the scent drawing him back to eating. Primarily he liked his jobs because he liked working with Audra, Jess, and Tom, not because of the work itself. He shrugged, not willing to put this into words.

"Well, you should give this some thought. Baking, or being a mechanic or law enforcement or… What do you want to do with your life, Chad?"

Chad chewed, giving consideration to what Harding had said. But was it realistic? For him? He'd never given the idea of a career any thought. An eagle swooping overhead cast its shadow over their table. Its shrill call broke the peace.

This must have triggered Harding. He jerked and glanced at his watch. "I've got to go soon. Do you have anything else we need to talk about?"

"No, I just hope you'll keep me in the loop. Not knowing is the worst."

Harding nodded solemnly.

"Jess said that when you gave her information about what she went through, it helped her."

"I'm glad we were able to help Jessie," Harding replied. "And I'll keep you in the loop. But I'll expect that whatever I tell you will go no further."

Chad recognized the serious tone Harding used. A thought came. "Right. I promise, but could I...could I share things with Jess? She's trustworthy."

Harding sent him an odd smile. "Jessie is that and more. Sure." The grin widened. "You can share anything I say with her. But just her."

Chad nodded and finished the last bite of his burger.

Harding did the same. His cell sounded and he began speaking to someone and gathering his trash. He left with a wave to Chad.

Chad munched the last of his fries, thinking over Harding's suggestion. *Me? A cop?* He shook his head. Not happening. He glanced at his watch and was soon in his truck, heading for Ashford Hospital. Me? A cop? But the suggestion had taken root in his mind. Was it even possible?

━━━

DOYLE HEARD HIMSELF GROAN—LOUD and long. The sound and the way it worked its way through his body woke him enough to blink his eyes. *Where am I?* He felt as if he was

45

coming off a drinking binge. *I never wanted, never thought I'd feel this way again—like I've been run over by a semi and then dragged behind it. Did I fall off the wagon?* He probed his memory and found nothing. Then the image of three men bursting into Uncle Dick's house blazed in his mind. *No.*

Did Uncle Dick need him? He struggled to get up and gazed around, still blinking. He braced an elbow against the hard floor to hold up his head. His neck felt like a cooked noodle. Then he felt something crusted on his forehead. He probed the area and found a wound and what must be dried blood. He wiped his palm over it and confirmed that it was dried blood. He tried to remember what had caused this wound, which was also swollen and painful to the touch, but his memory failed him.

He gazed around again. *Where am I?* His eyes cleared some more. He surveyed his surroundings. It looked like some kind of shed. The only light came from the slits around the door and one tiny window set high in the wall. He drew in a few deep breaths of warm stale air, trying to get enough strength to stand.

He managed to get onto his knees. He crawled to the wall and, pressing his hands against it, managed to rise. His head swam, but he pressed his forehead against the wall. That steadied him. What had happened to him? He knew he'd been knocked out. He recalled waking on the floor of a vehicle. And now he was here.

But what and where was here? He slowly turned, feeling wobbly and woozy. He gazed around at the shed's interior. It was empty except for some things bunched together on the floor by the door. He sucked in air and started creeping toward them, still keeping his hand against the wall.

When he reached the door, he tried to open it. He hadn't expected it to be unlocked. And it wasn't. He leaned down and examined the slit near the doorknob. He glimpsed evidence of more than one lock. So much for escape. His head pounded.

He looked down and saw a gallon jug of what looked like water, a bucket, and an energy bar. He glanced over his shoulder and saw that he'd also been left a blanket. Thirst hit him like a sledgehammer, making his dry throat gag. He opened the gallon jug and sniffed. It smelled like water. He stuck his finger in and then licked it. Water. He lifted the jug to his mouth and sucked in a long draft of the tepid liquid.

He put it down and carefully capped it. He rested his back against the door and gazed around his prison. He wished his mind wasn't so foggy. Again, it reminded him of the days that he'd spent drinking himself into oblivion and then suffering through the fog and pain of hangovers. But someone, not getting wasted, had done this. Who? Why? No answer came, but the feeling of being trapped triggered a spurt of dripping, icy fear. *Got to get out, get away.*

Maybe there were some loose boards or something. He began working his way around the four walls, pushing against them. Nothing budged. Finally he gave up. He made his way back to the energy bar and water. He could imagine what the bucket was for. How thoughtful. He slid the water jug along the floor with the toe of his shoe and then sat back down on his blanket. If it weren't for the cracks around the door, he wouldn't have anything stirring the stale air. *Oh, God, where am I? What's going on?*

Then he saw it on the floor—a scribbled note: He held it up to the slit of light from the door. BE READY TO TALK.

He gaped at it. Ready to talk? His hands shook as he opened the energy bar and bit into it. BE READY TO TALK? About what? To who? Fear sent an icy blast through him. Then he felt them, tears. He didn't try to stop them. Who would see them here? He lay down on the hard floor, as weak as a child, crying. *God, help.*

Chapter 6

Tamping down frustration, Chad had waited through all the time-consuming procedures of releasing Uncle Dick from the hospital. When they finally achieved freedom, he'd had to suppress the urge to press down on the gas pedal, to speed, to squeal out of the lot. But he'd reined himself in.

After commenting on how good the fresh air smelled, Uncle Dick didn't seem disposed to talk.

So Chad navigated the familiar roads home, unable to think of anything to say that might not upset the older man.

Finally Uncle Dick said, "I feel like I've been away for longer than a couple of days."

Chad, who had never stayed in the hospital, merely made a sound of acknowledgment. Reaching the familiar turnoff, he turned on his right blinker to head toward Uncle Dick's when his uncle stopped him.

"No, I'm not going back to my place."

What? Chad glanced sideways.

"Florence is going to put me up for a few days at her place. I just can't face..." Uncle Dick looked away, perhaps embarrassed by this admission.

Chad got it. Violence had desecrated his uncle's home, his safe place.

"I can't face not having Doyle there, you know?" The sadness in his voice touched, hit Chad harder than he'd expected. An invisible fist gripped his chest. Finally, he managed to reply, "I know." The words came out harsh.

Uncle Dick patted Chad's shoulder. "We'll get through this. I survived Korea. Losing my wife and son." He paused to swallow. "We'll get through this."

Sudden tears moistened Chad's eyes. He blinked them away.

Uncle Dick continued looking straight ahead. "Shirley has set up a bed for me in her dining room...said she doesn't use it anymore. I'll be eating at Shirley's just like Florence does, so you'll be seeing me more than usual."

Warm relief trickled through Chad. He'd contemplated moving in with Uncle Dick for a time. But this was better for his uncle. "I think that's good. Shirley's food's the best." *And Shirley and Tom are the best.*

"So Florence tells me." Uncle Dick chuckled. "You know, Florence and I grew up together. She was quite the tomboy. Her dad...wasn't worth much, but she had a good mom, and she married a good guy. It's too bad they never had kids."

All this was news to Chad. Usually he just thought of Florence as an old woman who rarely had a nice word to say. But that was probably because she didn't like his dad. But then who did? A glum thought.

Then he remembered that he was sitting by the man who'd defied all the advice and had helped his dad. In this moment, Chad resolved to do whatever was needed to repay this debt to his great uncle.

⊏⊐

JESSIE HAD OFFERED to help out with Audra's evening pizza business for her own reasons. When the evening was done, she wanted time alone with Chad as they walked home to their rooms at Shirley's. Time alone to find out how her suggestion that he talk with the sheriff had worked out. Had it helped or not? Jessie had refused to put the hours on the clock with Audra. Her boss had just smiled in an odd way at her when she'd said she was bored and working for free.

So Jessie boxed and carried pizzas to customers who appeared at the Dutch door. And in between chatted with Evie, now a teen, who liked to hang around the kitchen when she didn't have anything better to do. The twins were spending the evening with their father, who had taken them fishing. Down the street in the twilight, the sheriff had looked really happy, leading his two little boys with their short bamboo poles over their shoulders. It had touched Jessie's heart. She'd seen how stressed the sheriff was over what had happened at Dick's.

Finally Audra shut the Dutch door for the night and turned the answering machine on with its "Sorry you called too late" message. The three of them, with Evie's help, cleaned the kitchen so it would be ready for the morning bake. At last, Jessie and Chad left by the back door out onto the alley, quiet now in the night. Jessie drew in the clean lake air.

"You're wanting to ask me how it went with the sheriff," Chad said, his hands in his pockets and his face forward.

His listless tone didn't encourage her. She considered this and decided on just asking for more information. "What did the sheriff say?"

"Not much about the case that we already didn't know. Or that he hadn't announced on the radio today."

Jessie caught the note of irritation, kind of a seasoning on his simple answer. Chad didn't like any attention paid to his father. She could understand that. She could only imagine what having a father with such a dreadful reputation felt like.

Her parents might have kept her too close for her own good, but they were good people who loved her. Not able to think of words that wouldn't hurt him further, she reached over and patted his arm in sympathy.

His hand came up and pressed hers. A moment of closeness passed silently between them.

She was glad he was accepting, not shrugging off, her concern. She saw their bench just ahead. They often stopped here to talk. She hurried forward and he followed.

A sudden barking stopped them both. A German shepherd was barking and lunging against the chain-link fence around the backyard of the old Nielsen house. Mrs. Nielsen had passed over the winter. With no next of kin and several years of back taxes owed, the house had been auctioned off in May. A new owner had kept to himself while cleaning up the neglected yard and house. No one knew much about him.

At the violent barking, both Jessie and Chad halted in the middle of the alley. They heard the back door slam open and a large, silver-haired man hurried toward the dog. "What's going on out here?" he demanded.

"Nothing," Chad said, taking a step back, "we're just walking home."

"Where do you live?" the man asked, looking suspicious.

Jessie moved closer to Chad. "We live at Shirley and Tom Robson's house." She gestured toward the house about halfway up the alley.

"And," Chad added, "we work mornings and some evenings at Audra's Place." He gestured in the other direction. "I'm Chad Keski and this is Jessie Barnes."

"We weren't doing anything but walking," Jessie said. "Can we meet your dog? I hope he's not going to bark every night and disturb the neighborhood. You have Wilma's Bed and Breakfast right next door to you."

The older man studied them in the low light. "Don't want

to be a problem. Yeah, come over here and shake hands with me. Then King will know you're friends."

Jessie felt a bit nervous but went over and began talking to King and shook hands with the man. "What's your name, sir?"

"Greg Hawkins," he replied and said no more.

Chad shook hands and then both he and Jessie petted the dog. "Nice meeting you, Mr. Hawkins. Tom owns the garage on Main Street."

"Oh, I've heard good things about him."

"He's a good mechanic, a good guy. Well, nice to meet you." Chad tugged Jessie's elbow.

"Do you allow him doggie treats?" Jessie asked. "Sometimes Audra bakes special ones."

Mr. Hawkins studied them. Then he grinned. "That sounds like something I should investigate. But if you bring one by for him, call for me, or King won't touch it."

"A well-trained dog," Chad commented, drawing Jessie away. "Good night!"

The new neighbor wished them the same and King gave a different kind of bark in farewell.

Without a word, they both sat down on the old wooden bench that sat on the alley behind a house about three doors down from Shirley and Tom's place. The bench was hidden behind thick, high lilac bushes that were, of course, no longer in bloom. The house across from the bench and the houses on each side were also masked by either evergreens or more bushes.

Here in this small section of the alley, they were invisible to prying eyes. It wasn't that they couldn't talk at Shirley's but too many ears too close made them cautious. And Shirley didn't like them visiting each other in their rooms upstairs even though she knew they were just good friends. This bench was their place.

"So?" she prompted, settling herself in for a talk. Would he tell her all of it?

Chad cleared his throat. "He asked me if I knew of any of my dad's friends here."

She went over this in her mind before asking, "Does your dad have any friends around here?" In the quiet, a car passed by the end of the alley.

"No. The only group he goes to or belongs to is the AA group that meets every Wednesday night in Ashford."

"They would know your dad best. I mean, he goes every week and has for over two years." Someone nearby opened and then shut a door.

"But can they be considered friends?" A different, familiar dog, sounded like Shirley's, barked farther down the block and was hushed.

"I don't know, but why did the sheriff want to talk to your dad's friends? Wasn't it just to get more information about him?"

"I guess."

"Why don't we visit the group then? Does your dad have a sponsor or someone that he talks to?"

"Yeah, but I only know his first name. Barton."

"An interesting first name. Why don't we go to the next meeting, it's tomorrow, and see if Barton is there? And just ask for help." She sensed his reluctance to have anything to do with his father's alcoholism, the cause of all the troubles Doyle Keski had wreaked upon himself and Chad.

"I guess we could," he said, still sounding undecided.

He sounded so down she didn't know what to say next so she just waited to see if he had more to say.

"The sheriff said something odd to me."

She waited.

"He said...he said I ought to consider a career...in law enforcement."

This suggestion jolted her with surprise. "Wow. That's a real compliment."

"It's a joke," Chad replied with thick sarcasm. "Me? A cop?"

Without pausing to think, Jessie punched Chad's arm.

He glared at her. "What—"

"You'd make a great cop," she declared. "Why say it's a joke?"

He rubbed his arm though she knew she hadn't hurt him.

"Can you imagine people around here taking me seriously as a cop?"

Jessie paused, realizing her reply would mean something to Chad. She took her time drawing up her thoughts. "Chad, we're both living down narratives about us that people have crafted in their minds. I'm the amnesia girl—"

Chad tried to interrupt.

But she continued, "Yes, you're a Keski. Your grandfather and father both lived lives that won them disrespect or worse. But"—she held up her hand, forestalling him—"now you have a chance to change that narrative, to live your own life. Tom and Shirley came into your life and God came into your life. You are Chad Keski, not Doyle Keski. Yes, you could be a cop and a good one." She listened to more of the muted night sounds—distant voices on the nearby street, an owl hooting softly, the sound of the waves splashing against boats tethered in the marina a block away—giving him time to think.

━━

CHAD STARED AT JESS. Her words were spoken with power and confidence. He bowed his head and drew in her words deeply. He heard footsteps at the end of the alley, but they were heading away from them. Finally, he replied, "I'm tired of always bucking what you call my 'narrative.'"

"I get tired of mine too, but I'm going to outgrow it and change it. Why not do that together?" She rested her hand on top of his thigh, something she hadn't done before.

The simple yet intimate touch heightened his awareness of her to a new level. He swallowed, his throat suddenly dry. He thought of the sheriff's story. Sheriff Harding had changed his narrative. "Did you know that Harding nearly killed another teen in a fight at a drinking party?"

"Really?" Her tone rippled with shock. "I knew he was wild when he was young. Wow. That's a narrative I wouldn't want."

"Me either. But now he's sheriff."

"Yes, so why shouldn't you consider seriously what he suggested?"

Chad bent his head into his hands.

Jess patted him on the back.

He straightened up. "I will." He turned to her. "So should we go to my dad's AA group tomorrow?"

"Yes."

Chad gazed into her eyes, drawing strength from the support he saw there. Maybe going to the AA meeting would do nothing, but it was something to do to try to help his dad.

Jess rose and offered her hand.

He accepted it briefly and then they were heading home and as usual, talking to Jess made everything better. *She understands me.* It was a startling but good feeling.

JULY 13TH

Chad drove Jess to the church where the AA meeting took place. It was an old brick building on a street of older homes. He'd never been on this street before and he'd never felt curious about this place. He was just glad every time his dad made the drive to Ashford. Glad he didn't stop on the way at one of the bars.

"Nervous?" Jess asked after they met at the front of his truck in the sparsely populated parking lot.

"Don't know. I guess. I don't like talking to strangers." *And I don't like talking about what has happened to my dad.* Was he all right? Just thinking about it caused his heart to speed up. He drew in a deep, calming breath.

"Well, they can't eat us. And these are the only people that your dad has been with regularly for the past two years except for family. They might know something that might help the sheriff." She waited beside him.

He nodded and started toward the side entrance to the basement. A small temporary sign had directed them. He opened the door and let Jess precede him. They walked down a flight of stairs and heard voices coming from a room off to the side of the large open area with tables and what looked like a pass-through to a kitchen.

Jess headed toward the voices, opened the door, and stepped inside with Chad at her heels.

All those present fell silent and turned to stare at them.

"Hello," the man at the head of the table said. "You're late if you're here for the AA meeting."

"Sorry," Jess said. She looked to Chad.

Talk now or turn tail. "I'm Chad Keski. My dad is a member here, Doyle."

The men and women around the table continued staring at them.

"We wondered if the Doyle in the news who's missing is our Doyle," a gray-haired woman said. "Is there any news?"

"No. The sheriff asked me if my dad had any friends, and all I could think of was this group."

"The sheriff?" the middle-aged man at the head of the table asked.

"Yes," Jess said. "He's trying to find out any useful information about Chad's dad."

"I really don't think we can be much help," the same woman finally replied. "We don't talk about personal things, just our addiction and how to stay sober." The group nodded in agreement.

"I'm Barton, Doyle's sponsor," an older man with white hair offered. "Our meeting is almost finished. If you wait outside for me, I'll see if I can be of help."

Chad said his thanks and ushered Jess out to the warm night by the side entrance door. They only waited a few minutes before the AA members started coming out and going to their cars. Barton appeared near the end of the exodus and led them to a nearby bench.

"I really don't know much about your dad except what he's told me. I know about his out-of-control life, then his prison time and parole. He feels really bad about the way he let you down."

These words leaked into Chad's heart like warm cleansing water. He and his dad never talked about their troubled past. "Can you think of anything that would have prompted someone to kidnap him?"

Barton shook his head slowly. "I've already thought about it, trying to see if anything he said to me could be a reason he would be kidnapped. Honestly, nothing has come to mind. I'm sorry."

Chad nodded. "We're just trying anything we can think of."

Barton squeezed Chad's upper arm. "I'm praying for your dad. He's really come so far from where he was when he got out of prison. It's hard to believe that when he finally got control of his drinking and started living sober, something like this would happen."

Chad nodded at the same words he'd thought repeatedly

over the past few days.

By unspoken agreement, they all stood and headed toward their respective vehicles in the almost empty lot.

When Chad drove out onto the street, Jess patted his arm, but evidently even she couldn't think of anything comforting to say.

Chad's phone rang. He pulled it from his pocket and handed it to Jess to answer.

"It's the sheriff," she said.

Chad pulled over, accepted the phone, and put it on speaker. "Sheriff?" His voice cracked on the word.

"I need you to come to my office. We've found something we think might belong to your uncle Dick. It was found along the county road that the assailants used on their way out. Can you come now?"

Chad assented and then pulled back onto the street.

Again Jess said nothing but rested a hand on his thigh. Her touch comforted him. He tried to quell the urge to hope. But it bobbed up inside him even as he struggled. He glanced sideways and saw that Jess's head was bowed, no doubt praying about what they'd find in Winfield.

Chapter 7

July 13th

Anxiety gnawing at him, Chad had driven them straight to the sheriff's office in Winfield. Now Jess walked beside him through the early night to the sheriff's department door. He let himself reach for her hand. He was so glad to have Jess at his side, in his life. With each new lead, the same sensation flooded him. He didn't like the feeling of being exposed, worried and uncertain. Her presence, her hand in his, helped him face this new thing, whatever it might be.

Soon they entered the sheriff's office. He waved them to sit in the two chairs on the opposite side of his desk. Just as the sheriff started to speak, Uncle Dick and Florence joined them. At the sight of Florence at Uncle Dick's side, Chad's mood sank like a rock. Why was she here? Still, he rose politely and gave his seat to Florence.

Jess rose and motioned toward the other chair for Uncle Dick.

Chad stood leaning against the wall, facing the sheriff. His grim expression felt hard, like it was set in concrete. Jess took her place at his side. That helped.

After polite greetings, Harding said, "I'll get right down to it." He then lifted a large paper grocery bag from the floor. With gloved hands, he slid out a battered gray metal box about the size of two loaves of bread, side by side. "A couple of volunteers were cleaning up the roadside about two miles from your place, Dick. They found this several feet from the roadside among a thicket of ferns. Someone must have thrown it really hard. I'm surprised my officers missed it, but…" He shrugged.

"Nobody's perfect," Uncle Dick muttered.

"Do you recognize this box?" Harding asked, still holding it up.

"Sure. I keep cash in it. I don't like using those ATM cards. I like cash on hand."

"Did you have it where anyone could easily find it?" The sheriff gazed at Uncle Dick.

His uncle nodded once with force. "In my desk in the living room. I do my paperwork there, you know, pay bills and keep track of expenses."

"We found both your prints and Doyle's on it and some smudged ones that we couldn't identify." Harding set it on his desk.

"Why were Doyle's prints on it, Dick?" Florence interrupted, her voice suspicious.

Chad gritted his teeth so he wouldn't say what he thought of this question.

"Sometimes when we were heading to town, I'd ask Doyle to get money out for us," Uncle Dick answered, letting her see with his frown that he didn't appreciate her question.

"Humph." Florence let the sound show her own disapproval.

Uncle Dick patted her arm and murmured, "Relax."

"Did you have any cash in it this week?" Harding asked.

Chad appreciated that the sheriff was keeping his tone non-committal. He wasn't piling on his dad.

"Yeah, a couple hundred dollars." Uncle Dick let out a sound of disgust. "So they got that."

"You mean your good-for-nothing nephew got it," Florence growled.

Before Chad could think how or whether to react to this, his uncle turned on her. "Flo, that's enough about Doyle. They knocked him out before they came after me. He tried to defend me, but he's not a big man and there were three of them."

His uncle's defense of his father lifted Chad's mood.

Still pressing her lips together, Florence bowed her head. "Okay."

"Doyle has changed over the past two years, Flo," Uncle Dick declared. "It's been slow and hard-won. But he's only slipped once this year and after one drink, he got himself out of the bar and headed home before he had too much to drive. No one's perfect, Flo. But I'm tired of everyone harping on me about this. Do you think if he wasn't getting better I would have kept him with me for over two years? Do you think I'm stupid?" Uncle Dick's voice rose as his defense continued.

His face had become red and Chad moved forward and squeezed his shoulder. "Chill, Uncle Dick. It's okay. I know what everyone always says about my dad. But he has been different since he started living with you. I see it."

"So do I," Jess seconded.

"So have I," Harding agreed.

"Well," Florence said obviously still unconvinced, "I'll stop speaking against him then. No, Dick, you aren't stupid. But after knowing both Chad's grandfather and father, it's hard to let go of the old. And this has just stirred up the history around here. I won't repeat it, but you know what people will say when they hear about this metal box and the money missing."

"I don't intend that anyone will hear about this, Florence," Harding said, his tone carrying a warning. "This evidence is not going to be revealed until I know how it all fits. This is not a simple case. We still don't know why the attackers took Chad's father with them or what the real purpose of all this was. I can't think a few hundred dollars was the motive."

Florence nodded slowly. "No one will hear it from me. My word." She looked to Uncle Dick and nodded once as if in emphasis.

After this, there wasn't much more to say. The box was Uncle Dick's. It had contained two hundred dollars and could have been easily found by the intruders.

Chad couldn't think what this added to their information about his uncle being assaulted and his father being taken. Which was almost nothing.

Following Uncle Dick and Florence to the parking lot, Chad and Jess walked, hand in hand, to his truck and drove off, heading in the same direction as the older couple, heading home.

Once again Jess rested a hand on his thigh. Her touch comforted him more than he wanted to acknowledge. He glanced from the corner of his eye and was caught by how lovely she was. Her pale skin shone in the darkness. Were the men around here crazy? Then an unexpected feeling of possessiveness blindsided him. He didn't want any man noticing how special Jess was. As he drove toward Shirley's, he tried to digest this new reaction.

JESSIE SAT BESIDE CHAD, hoping her presence alone comforted him. When would all this horrible disaster end? Just one thing after another. And how would it end? Sudden fear riddled her. Again she rested her hand on Chad's thigh. She felt the need again to connect to him. She wondered when the physical barrier between them had begun to dissolve. Did friends of opposite sexes rest hands on thighs? But the gesture had come so naturally. Touching Chad told him without words that she was with him in this. He wasn't alone. She drew in a long breath. Maybe it was time to acknowledge that their relationship was entering a new, deeper level. Everything that hurt him hurt her too, but more, much more, than it had before.

She groped for words. But she couldn't find any that expressed what she was feeling. Or that she wanted to say aloud to Chad. *Oh, dear Lord, please help Chad. Help his dad. Why can't we get any leads to where he is? It's been three days.*

Without questioning herself, she leaned her head on Chad's arm and, as they reached town, gazed out at the streetlights parading past the truck window.

"I don't want to go home right now," Chad said, his voice very low, very soft.

She lifted her head and waited for him to go on.

"I think I want to walk down by the wharf. It will be quiet there. I can think."

"You want to go alone?" she asked.

"Yes." But he touched her hand that still lay on his thigh.

She recognized the gesture of reassurance. "I understand," she replied. And she did. Sometimes a person had to be alone to think. "Anyway I need to go to Audra's kitchen and work on my dough for tomorrow morning. I'm going to let it rise overnight again. People loved the sour taste it added."

"I know. I'll drop you off there." He drove the last few blocks to the alley behind Audra's.

She reached down for her purse. He climbed out and came over to open the door for her, something he rarely did when it was just the two of them. She slid down to the ground and then gazed at him. The air around them felt charged with some special significance. She didn't want to spoil it by speaking. So she moved against him and rested her head on his T-shirt.

He stroked her back and then kissed the top of her head. "See you tomorrow."

She nodded against him, then stepped away and hurried through the gate and to the back door. She unlocked it and listened as Chad drove away. Inside, she stood for several moments, remembering the feel of Chad's shirt under her cheek. *He kissed my head.* Yes, everything was changing. And since this was Chad, the old fear of getting close to someone didn't rear up. *I know Chad.*

Turning away from these thoughts, she hung up her purse and washed her hands, trying to move her mind to the job at hand. Her artisan bread was selling well, very well. An old love song came to mind, something her dad always sang to her mother when he was being romantic. She smiled and hummed it. And then said a prayer for Chad and his father.

CHAD HAD ALWAYS LOVED the quiet of the wharf at night and now more than ever before. The waves slapping the hulls of the boats moored there was a comforting rhythm. The gulls had quieted for the night and humans had done the same, seeking their comfortable chairs inside. At the other end of the wharf, another lone soul paused to stare out at the water. Chad didn't begrudge the stranger the peace of this place, but he moved in the opposite direction. He didn't want to talk to anyone. Hearing his own footsteps was a solitary sound. In the morning this wharf would once again be clogged with tourists. What a contrast.

Chad couldn't believe he'd kissed Jess's head. But he'd merely done what he felt moved to do. Jess was so special and so loyal. *I can count on Jess.* And she could count on him. It was a good feeling, warming him inside.

Then the scene at the sheriff's office intruded. The metal

box. Did it mean anything? Other than that the men who'd attacked Uncle Dick and kidnapped his father had taken it and when they felt like it, they had opened it and taken the cash out, then tossed it away? He recalled Florence's reaction, and it ground inside him like shards of glass. No matter what his father had done to clean up his life, who in town believed that he was an innocent victim?

I do, Chad said to himself. His father was doing well. He actually smiled sometimes, something he'd never done when Chad was a child—at least in a good way. The old Doyle Keski had only smiled in a nasty way just before he said or did something to hurt someone.

Chad paused and sat down on a hard bench on the edge of the wharf. Not for the first time, he thanked God for Shirley taking him in as her foster child. He recalled some flashes of memory from that rough first year at her place. He hadn't trusted her. He'd defied her. Yet she had quietly won his respect. She had proved herself different from everyone else in town. She'd given him a chance to separate himself from his dad.

When he'd realized that she was getting close to Tom, who'd been boarding in her house, he hadn't liked it at all. But Tom too had slowly won his respect and then affection. Chad bowed his head, acknowledging how much he owed them, a debt they never asked to be repaid. He vowed again that he would be here for them whenever they needed him.

Then his conversation with Harding came to mind. The sheriff had suggested he study law enforcement. As Chad thought about this, he didn't have the same reaction he had initially. Could he do that? Jess thought so. When he'd graduated from high school, both Shirley and Tom had urged him to go to the local community college, but he'd refused. He'd been happy to just continue working for Audra and Tom.

Now the idea of a career had been planted and it was

starting to sprout within him. For the first time, he suddenly felt as if he could come out from behind his father's shadow, fully out. And Jess came to mind. His chest tightened when he thought of her at his side. She'd become his best friend and vice versa, but matters between them were changing in just three days.

He'd always been very careful not to cross the invisible line she'd etched around herself. She'd never accepted offers of dates with other guys. And he'd been happy just to be her friend. But now he saw that they might be more. In the future. When all this had come right. Come right? Where had that phrase come from? How could this situation with his dad come right?

———

DOYLE WOKE to the slam of a car door. He lay on the blanket, drenched with sweat and smelling his own body odor. The jug of water was almost empty and his stomach was hollow. The single energy bar had been all he'd eaten for almost three days now.

He heard voices. Someone or someones were coming. Fear grabbed him around the chest.

BE READY TO TALK.

He stared in the darkness at the door. Would he finally find out who had kidnapped him? And why? Fear gripped him tighter.

BE READY TO TALK.

His teeth started to chatter, and he clamped his jaw together. Fear enveloped his whole body. *I'm so weak.* He lifted the water or what was left of it to his mouth. He'd saved some so when "they" came, he'd be able to talk. He gritted his teeth against the persistent vertigo and made himself sit up and then get on his feet. He couldn't show fear. He knew how intimidation worked. He drew in a deep breath and faced the door.

BE READY TO TALK.

Chapter 8

The door locks were clicked and released. The door swung back with a bang. Fresh cooling night air rushed in. Two men entered, filling the doorway and halting. Doyle tried to study them, but the scant moonlight behind them revealed only two large shapes. They just stood and stared at him.

He fought the urge to ask them anything. He was desperate to know who they were and why he was here. But he couldn't sound desperate. He would wait and see what they said, hoping they would give him some clue to their identity.

He studied what he could see of them in the dimness. Then a thought occurred to him. Did he want to recognize them? Would they let him live if he could ID them? He drew in the warm air and tried to keep himself steady on his feet.

The minutes crawled by. Sweat trickled down Doyle's back. An unseen whippoorwill broke the silence, calling out its name over and over.

Finally, a voice behind the two figures said, "So, Keski, are you ready to talk?"

Doyle listened carefully. Did the distinctive voice sound familiar? Maybe. He took his time answering the question.

Finally, when one of the figures moved forward, Doyle said, "About what?"

"You have information we want," the same faceless voice said.

"Oh?" Doyle said, trying to sound nonchalant.

"Quit messing with us," one of the large men in front of him barked. "We're getting—"

The unseen speaker cut in. "You had a cellmate who died in the cell with you." It wasn't a question.

His words took Doyle back to the worst of those awful prison nights, the one he wished he could forget. But that one had been the night that had begun the change in him. He'd never forget the terror of his cellmate, Getz, as he realized he was dying. The fear of death. Stark terror. Chilled by the memory, Doyle swallowed to keep his voice calm. "Yeah, what about it?"

"We know cellmates talk," the voice prompted.

Doyle again let the silence build. When the figures in front of him began fidgeting, he spoke. "He told me exactly nothing, nothing but complaints about the food, about how nobody visited him, about his lousy lawyer—"

"Not interested in crap." The voice cut him off. "When people are about to die, they talk. Tell secrets. Getz had information he knew we'd need. We want it. What did he tell you?"

Again Doyle's mind took him back to that wretched night with him calling for the guards and Getz gripping his shirt front, saying over and over, "I don't want to go to hell."

Then Doyle concentrated on the present. If he told them he knew nothing, what would they do? Would they believe him? An owl hooted in the distance.

"If you're not ready to talk, we can come back," the voice said ominously.

"I don't have anything to tell you," Doyle said, deciding telling the truth might be best.

"Don't have anything you will tell, or you don't know anything?"

"Getz just kept saying he didn't want to go to hell. That's it."

A long silence ensued. Fear arced through Doyle in throbbing icy waves. What would they do now? Would they let him go? Or...

"I don't believe you," the voice said. "I think you need more time to probe your memory. Getz wasn't the best at keeping a secret. Do what we planned," he said to the two men blocking the door.

What they planned? Doyle sucked in air.

The two men barged in.

Terror nearly lifted him from the floor. Doyle stumbled backward.

He couldn't see what they were doing, but they were gone within minutes, slamming and locking the door behind them. The sound sank deep within him. Blackness enveloped him, almost smothering him. He waited where he was, listening to the vehicle drive away. They'd done something with the bucket by the door. His hands reaching in front of him, he felt his way through the blackness and finally, felt the rough wooden door ahead of him.

His toe touched the odorous bucket and it nearly tipped. They must have emptied it. He felt farther with his toe and found a new jug. He lowered himself to his knees and opened it. More water. He felt around the jug. He found it, what he really needed. Relief oozed through him. Another energy bar. He sat down and opened the bar's wrapper. Though ravenous, he'd only eat a bite and then save it in his pocket. So they were keeping him alive till he remembered.

Remembered what? And what if he had nothing to tell them? How would they accept that fact the next time they came?

Over the past years he had fought the alcohol addiction that had ruled him since his teens. Being sober had given him back control over his life. Every sober day had been difficult, but the freedom from bleary, lost nights and wretched mornings had been sweet. His son's face came to mind. For the first time his son had actually wanted to spend time with him. Doyle groaned. Would he ever see him again?

JULY 14TH

With a start, Chad woke on the bench by the wharf. *I must have been more tired than I thought.* He got up, looked around in the scant moonlight and then rubbed his bare arms. It got chilly by the water after dark. Waves still lapped the hulls of the nearby boats.

In the silent night, he turned and headed toward home, across the street and then up the alley past Audra's, then Tom's garage and finally to Shirley and Tom's place. Not another sound, only his footsteps and a dog that barked twice as Chad passed his yard. He opened the back gate and felt for his key ring in his pocket.

A faint voice stopped him. Had he imagined it? He waited...

"Help," came the exhausted-sounding voice.

Chad waited and listened for the voice again. Had he imagined it?

"Help."

He turned toward the voice. It was Florence's. He ran down the alley and through the gate right next to Shirley's. He hurried into Florence's backyard. And up to the back door. "Florence," he called quietly, not wanting to disturb the surrounding houses unless necessary.

"Help. I'm upstairs and can't get off the floor." Her weak voice was barely audible.

He tried her door. Locked.

"It's Chad. I'll climb through a window. I'm coming."

"Pleeeaaase."

He went around the first floor and found an open window. He lifted out the screen and hoisted himself up and over the sill. "I'm in, Florence. Where are you?"

"Outside the upstairs bathroom."

He headed up the stairs and by the light of a few night-lights found the older woman in faded men's pajamas, sprawled on the floor.

"I slipped and hurt my elbow." She nodded toward her right side. "And twisted my ankle." She nodded to her left side. "So I couldn't put weight on either side." She stifled a sob. "I've been lying here for hours."

"Florence, I'm going to call Tom."

"Yes, call him."

Tom answered and, after a brief explanation, Chad ended the call. "Florence, I'm going to go down and open the back door for him. He's coming right over."

Florence grabbed his arm. "Thank you. I'm hurting."

He patted her hand like he'd seen Shirley do and then headed down the stairs. He barely got the door open and Tom was there, jeans pulled on over his pajama pants.

"She's upstairs and she can't get onto her feet," Chad said. "I didn't want to try to get her up by myself. I didn't want her to fall again."

"Good thinking, Chad." The two of them hurried up the stairs. "I'm here, Florence," Tom said. He knelt in the tight hallway next to her. "Where do you hurt?"

"My ankle." She pointed to the one that even Chad saw was swollen. "And my elbow." She lifted it and smothered a moan.

Tom gently examined the elbow and ankle, making Florence moan more than once. "I think we better call for an ambulance—"

"No!" Florence exclaimed.

"Florence, I think your elbow might be just a sprain but your ankle... I think it's broken. Now, let's not make the situation worse than it is. I'll tell them they don't need a siren. Just to come and take you to the hospital." He pulled out his cell and began talking to the 911 dispatcher.

Florence started crying.

Chad patted her shoulder awkwardly. "I know. I hate hospitals too."

She grabbed his hand and pressed it to her cheek. "I'm so glad you came. You just don't know...lying here...alone..." She wept harder.

Startled, Chad let her hold his hand and kept patting her shoulder with the other. Florence LaVesque was not his favorite person, but he could sympathize with her feelings of helplessness and pain. "Help's coming," he murmured. "It'll be okay."

She nodded, still weeping.

Tom ended the call. "Chad's right. We'll get you taken care of, Florence."

Then Shirley appeared at the bottom of the steps. Chad moved away and let Shirley take over comforting her longtime neighbor.

By the time Florence was carried down to the ambulance parked in the alley, Chad realized he just had time for a shower before he headed to Audra's. *It's good I napped at the wharf,* he said to himself.

Shirley climbed into the ambulance to go with Florence. After Tom helped Chad replace the screen, the two of them headed back to get a few more.

"How did you hear Florence?" Tom asked.

"I fell asleep on a bench by the seawall and was just opening our gate when I heard her voice."

"Deep thinking down at the wharf, huh?" Tom sent Chad a sideways glance as they quietly mounted the porch steps to their own back door.

"Yeah," Chad admitted.

"Want to talk about it?" Tom asked in a near whisper as they passed through the kitchen. Both of them were very aware of Uncle Dick snoring softly in the nearby dining room.

"Not now," Chad whispered back, not ready to talk about it yet, not even to Tom. "No time. I need to shower and get to Audra's."

"And I need some more sleep." The two of them parted at Tom and Shirley's bedroom door on the second floor. "I'm really glad you heard Florence." Tom squeezed Chad's shoulder like he did whenever he was pleased with him.

"Me too." Chad went into his room opposite to gather his clothes for the day. When he stepped back into the hall, he halted in surprise.

Jess stood at the bottom of the narrow flight of stairs that led up to the attic where her room was. "What's wrong?" she asked in a whisper. "I heard doors opening downstairs."

Chad explained and tried not to stare at her. In the low light, she stood there with her hair rumpled and clutching a cotton print robe around her pajamas, modestly dressed. But he rarely saw her, really never saw her like this—just out of bed, natural and soft-looking. He reined himself in. And focused on her face. Which also beckoned him to come closer.

"I need to shower and head to Audra's," he said.

She nodded, yawning. "I'll see you later then." She turned and then turned back, surprising him with a peck on the cheek. "That's for helping Florence." Then she hurried up the steps, her slippers slapping on each stair tread.

He finally broke out of a kind of trance and headed for the

bathroom across the hall. These new feelings for Jess were getting harder to ignore. Did she feel them too?

JESSIE STOOD at the top of the steps in the open area there. Her heart pounded, not from running up the stairs, but…

Why did I kiss Chad?

She entered her large room that spanned most of the attic. Sitting down on the side of her bed, she gathered her knees to herself and folded her arms around her knees as if taking control of herself.

Why did I kiss Chad?

It wasn't much of a kiss. Just a peck.

That didn't match how it had felt when her lips touched his stubbly cheek. She drew in a long breath. And buried her head against her pajamaed thighs. Some kind of landslide was going on inside her. Everything was moving around and feelings she hadn't felt for years, hadn't ever wanted to feel again, were bubbling up like an unexpected spring.

But I'm not afraid.

She'd kissed him because he'd fallen asleep at the wharf, watching the moonlight on the water, he'd said. And he'd come home and then helped Florence. Helped the woman who never had a kind word to say about his dad. Or to Chad himself, now that she thought about it. It only proved what she'd known all along. Chad Keski was underestimated by everyone but Audra's family and Tom and Shirley. And God. She resolved then not to let Chad underestimate himself. No, she wouldn't!

Chapter 9

July 15th

After lunch the next day, Chad and Jess were helping Shirley prepare her first-floor dining room to take in another resident. Florence's broken ankle had been encased in a cast and she was coming home from the hospital today. Audra and her mother, Lois, had already left for the hospital to bring Florence home. Shirley had decided that her neighbor would need help and it would be more convenient to give it to her here. Plus, Uncle Dick would be company for her.

Chad wondered what the prickly Florence would have to say about this decision, but Shirley had made the decision, not him. His mind drifted from Florence to the person she never missed an opportunity to diss, his dad. Not knowing what had happened to his father tried to take over his mind. He'd resisted panicking but four days had gone by. How many more? Where was Doyle? What were the chances...

To distract himself, he climbed the ladder with a sturdy cup hook in one hand. Shirley had decided to hang a curtain between the bed for Florence and the one already there, Uncle Dick's. So Chad was doing his part to separate the two halves of the room. He'd already twisted one cup hook on the other side of the room.

Uncle Dick hovered in the background, giving encouragement and fretting. "I don't know what Florence will say when you bring her here," he said for the third time, voicing Chad's worry.

"She will probably fuss," Shirley answered again, directing Chad where she wanted the second cup hook inserted in the plastered wall. "But actually I think she'll be relieved. If she had any family left nearby, it would be different. But she doesn't, and we've lived side by side for over forty years. I think that makes us as close as family."

"Yes, No family and no children. I know she wanted children," Uncle Dick added. "We dated, you know, in high school."

Chad tried to imagine anyone wanting to date the sharp-spoken woman and failed.

"She was quite a looker then and so sassy." Uncle Dick chuckled. Then he frowned. "It's hard getting old and living alone," he said under his breath.

Chad was glad that Uncle Dick hadn't been alone. Chad and his dad had drawn closer to to his uncle over the past three years.

"This curtain will provide some privacy for you both," Jess said as she finished clipping metal curtain rings onto a large light blue bedsheet. Then she slid the rings onto a clothesline that had already been secured to the first hook.

"Well, I just hope Flo will see it that way," Uncle Dick said.

Chad finished twisting the second cup hook into the plaster wall to hold the other end of the curtain.

"And it won't be for long," Shirley went on. "Just till we get a bedroom set up in her own downstairs dining room and she gets used to her cast. Also, I'm so glad that a few years ago she had the forethought to add a shower in her laundry room behind the kitchen. So she has the equivalent of a full bath downstairs. I think she's going to have to get used to living on one level."

Uncle Dick humphed, registering one last objection. "Florence is mighty independent."

"You mean stubborn," Shirley teased. "But she's also a realist, Dick. She'll do what she has to in order to stay safe and out of the hospital."

"Besides," Chad added, trying to lighten the mood, "she likes Shirley's cooking."

Uncle Dick laughed out loud at this observation. Chad couldn't help smiling. It was good to hear his great uncle laugh.

They all knew that for over two years, Florence had been eating regularly at Shirley's table and paid her a small monthly stipend for this service. Before that, she'd "just happen" to drop in as the family was sitting down to dinner. Often. Finally, Shirley had asked her to come every day, and Florence had insisted on paying her.

Reaching overhead, Jess handed Chad the end of the clothesline with the sheet attached, and Chad finished twisting and tying the clothesline firmly to the cup hook before coming down the ladder. "Done."

Shirley beamed at him. "Thanks so much, Chad. I didn't want Tom to have to miss work to help me do this. He's so busy this summer."

"Chad's always ready to help me too," Uncle Dick said. "Lots of young guys don't care anything about family."

Shirley walked over to Chad and kissed his forehead, something she did when she was pleased with him.

"It's no big deal," he mumbled and then glanced at the wall clock. "Time for me to head over to Tom's." He turned to say something to Jess, and her expression stopped him in his tracks. She was glaring at him, really glaring. What about?

━━

JESSIE FUMED in silence and hoped no one else noticed her mood. Once again, Chad blew off someone's thanks for his help and approval. She knew why, of course. Almost all his life he'd been put down because of his father and even grandfather.

This had to change, and only Chad could change it. And if no one else would say that to him, she would.

She remembered her counselor telling her that people would treat her the way she expected them to. Her parents had loved and protected her so much that she hadn't done much on her own. She hadn't developed self-confidence from her own life experiences and successes. That had been one contributing cause for what had happened to her two years ago, why she had ended up here, lying unconscious in the snow. Thank God Lois had found her.

The front door opened. "We need help!" Audra's mom called in.

Chad hurried to help Audra get Florence and her crutches up the four porch steps to Shirley's door.

Dick waited just inside the door, encouraging his longtime friend. Shirley led them into her living room where she'd set up one of her dining room chairs that had arms for Florence. "I knew a chair like this would be best for you, Florence," Shirley said as she bent to hug her.

Florence set aside her crutches and lowered herself onto the cushioned chair. She leaned her head into her hand.

"How about a Coke?" Dick asked.

She looked up at him. "That sounds wonderful. Lots of ice too."

Dick chuckled as he turned toward the kitchen. "Comin' up, Flo."

"I'm exhausted," she admitted. "Why do they have so

many hoops you have to jump through just to get out of the hospital?"

"It's one of those mysteries of life," Lois replied, sitting on the sofa opposite Florence. Everyone found a seat except for Chad, who stood in the doorway.

"I'm glad you finally got through all their hoops," Jessie said.

Chad glanced at his watch. "I have to head over to Tom's now."

Dick came back, carrying a tall frosty glass of Coke. "For you." He handed it to Florence with a napkin.

"Thanks again, Chad, for coming to help me last night," Florence said, raising her head. "I could have been lying there a lot longer."

Dick nodded, murmuring agreement. "I hate to think of you like that, Flo."

Chad shrugged. "No problem. If I hadn't fallen asleep at the wharf, I'd have been in bed."

"I'm glad you fell asleep at the wharf then," Florence said with a smile on her face and in her voice.

"Okay," Chad said, obviously uneasy with this praise. "I'll be home with Tom for supper."

Irritated even more, Jessie moved toward him. "I'll walk you."

Chad nodded and the two of them walked down the hall and out the back door.

Jessie was still fuming but trying to calm herself.

"So what's bugging you?" Chad asked in an undertone.

Jessie's patience snapped. "You are bugging me."

Chad halted. "Why? What did I do?"

"Why can't you," she demanded, also stopping, "accept thanks when they're deserved?" Her hands fisted on her hips.

His face twisted into a frown and he stared at her. "What?"

"Why can't you accept thanks when they're deserved?" she repeated, leaning forward.

He shook his head at her as if shaking off rain and started walking again.

She saw their bench ahead. She took his arm and steered him to it. "We're talking about this. Now. I'm done with you carrying around your family's bad rep like a load of garbage on your back. You are Chad Keski, not Harold or Doyle Keski. You are you."

He looked away.

She reached over and grabbed his chin and turned his face toward her. "Why didn't you just accept Shirley's and Dick's and Florence's thanks? You deserved their thanks, and it was right that they expressed it. Why can't you accept a compliment?"

He pursed his lips and tugged free of her hand.

"Answer me."

He thrust his chin out. "I didn't do anything special. You would have done the same."

"Yes," she said, jutting her chin closer to his, "but I would have been gracious enough to accept their thanks. Not tell them"—she continued in a mocking tone—"'It was nothing, no big deal.' When you don't accept gratitude with grace, it shouts that you're suffering from low self-esteem."

Their noses less than an inch apart, Jessie stared into his eyes and he stared back.

"What's going on here?" he asked in an undertone, sounding confused and a bit hurt. "What's got into you?"

She grabbed his upper arms. And squeezed. "You," she whispered. "You're getting to me. You've been a great friend, but now…"

"What?"

His pained tone prodded her. "Now I'm feeling more." The words came out in an explosive burst. "I never thought…I could…" She let go of his arms and then cupped his cheek. "I'm starting to feel more for you. Chad…more…"

Again they stared into each other's eyes, frozen in place, both breathing as if they'd been running.

Two kids on bikes burst into the alley, laughing and good-naturedly trashing each other.

Jessie dropped her hand from Chad's cheek and they moved apart.

The kids flashed past their bench, leaving them alone in the alley once more.

"You mean that?" Chad asked, his voice low and his tone raw.

"Yes." She spoke with firm purpose but faced forward. "Even if you don't feel anything for me."

Chad's hand sought hers. "I've been feeling something…too."

They gripped one another's hands. She knew she couldn't force another word out. She'd taken the lead and she was spent. Shock at her own boldness rippled through her in waves.

"I've got to go," Chad said, rising and looking confused.

She rose too. "I need to go back and help Shirley."

Chad gave her a funny little wave and hurried away.

Hearing her furry friend King barking for her to come pet him, she turned, the rapid pulsing from her impetuous declaration still coursing through her. *I didn't mean to say that now.*

———

FROM BELOW A LATE model car raised on the hoist above his head, Chad stared up at the undercarriage. But all he was seeing was the image of Jess's face when she'd said, "I'm starting to feel more for you…"

A kind of bubbling was going on inside his body. And his mind was a jumble of thoughts and feelings. He'd suffered through a few doomed crushes in high school and that had taught him to have no illusions about what people around here thought of him as a prospective boyfriend.

"Is there something I can help you with?" Tom's voice came from the left side. "You've been staring at that undercarriage for about five minutes."

His words jerked Chad back to the present. "Sorry. My mind was wandering."

Tom's face appeared. "Are you worrying about your dad?"

The reminder tipped Chad into gloom. He stared at Tom. "Some." The by now familiar and unwelcome feeling of helplessness wrapped around his lungs. Where was his dad? Was he hurt? Dead? For a moment he couldn't draw a breath.

Bending his head, Tom reached under the suspended car and touched Chad's shoulder. "It's times like these that test our faith. God knows where your dad is, and we're all praying for his safe return."

Chad nodded. For a moment he wanted, really wanted, to discuss what Jess had said to him only minutes before with this understanding man. But it was too new, too private, even for Tom. "I know. I'll get started. Keep busy."

"Good." Tom walked away, his shoes quiet on the concrete floor. "Keeping busy always helps me when I'm worried."

Chad began working on the car. The wrench in his hand felt solid. So different from his emotions that still swayed and swelled inside him. Then another phrase Jess had barked at him surfaced: "When you don't accept gratitude with grace, it shouts that you're suffering from low self-esteem." Self-esteem —social workers and school counselors had said that phrase over and over to him. But he'd heard more than once at church that no one was supposed to "think more highly of themselves than they ought." Well, how was a person supposed to do both? Have self-esteem but not think too much of one's self?

His brain hurt from trying to twist itself around the contradiction.

He couldn't forget what Jess had said. That he should stop living under his father's bad rep and that she was beginning to have feelings for him, not just friendship. He'd believed that only he had been feeling this change in their friendship. *But it's not just me.* The idea shook him to his heart. But in a good way —scary, but good. Still the old feelings of being less closed in around him like a swarm of mosquitoes. He took a deep breath and concentrated on the task at hand. He'd think about this when he could handle it.

Then once again the raw horror of his father's disappearance swept everything else away. The hard concrete in the pit of his stomach made itself known once more. *Help my dad. Help, please.*

———

DOYLE'S own voice woke him. He lay sweat-drenched, twisted in his blanket on the hard floor. He lay on his back, spent. His second night after the last visit by his captors. "I've lived some awful days," he muttered to the darkness, "but these have been some of the worst in my whole life."

He gazed up in the dark veil all around him. Though he didn't want it to, his mind dragged him back to the last night of Getz's life. The guy hadn't been that old, looked younger than Doyle. But anyone could see he'd lived a hard life, harder than most. Doyle had never been interested enough to find out what Getz had been convicted of. The man had been covered with tats and was intimidating in size. His guess had been drug trafficking charges. So common in prison.

The energy bar was gone and his empty stomach growled. Doyle pulled himself up into a sitting position and rested his head in his hands. "How'm I going to get out of this?" he asked the empty air. He'd gone over and over everything Getz had said, but the man had told him nothing that would answer the questions put to him last night. Even years later the memory of Getz's stark terror at dying sent chills up his spine. Doyle had never thought much about hell, but the fear of hell had pushed him into taking AA seriously.

Tears leaked from his eyes. He held his head in his hands, broken. "God, I know what I am. I've lived a worthless life—a bad husband and a bad father, a bad everything." He sucked in his tears and coughed. "Shirley and Tom keep telling me that You love me. And I don't deserve anything from You. But think of Chad." He voiced the worry that plagued him the most, "If they kill me and no one ever finds my body, it will hurt him bad, real bad. So help me, please, to get through this…somehow. For my son. I failed him so bad after his mother died…" Another sob choked off his words and he let the weeping overtake him.

JULY 16TH

In the middle of last night—a sleepless one, Chad had come to a decision. The realization that Jess had feelings for him packed power strong enough to move him to act. He was driving north now after his shift at Audra's. He had time and an urgent reason to find out if he could actually set a different course for his life. He drew in a deep breath as he rounded the last forested curve to his destination. *Dear Lord, I don't know if I can do this. Help me.*

Chapter 10

July 17th

The next morning very early in Audra's kitchen, Chad followed his usual routine and rolled out the proved sweet dough for the cinnamon rolls. He loved the feel of the springy dough in his hands. He glanced at the large old-fashioned round clock on the wall, gauging how soon Jess would come through the back door to work on her own bread dough. He was proud of her. Her breads sold out every day. Everything in the quiet kitchen around him was business as usual. But the churning he felt inside was anything but usual. His every sense was tuned to listening for Jess's arrival.

The sound he was waiting for came—the key turning in the lock, the door opening, the sound of the crows in the alley cawing.

Letting in summer, Jess entered and shut the door behind her. "Morning, Chad."

For a moment he couldn't speak. How could the sound of her voice tie him up inside? He drew in air bit by bit. "Same to you," he managed to say.

Dressed as usual in a T-shirt and jeans, Jess seemed to light up the room. She glanced at him and cocked her head to one side. "Everything okay?"

He had hoped to delay telling her what he'd done yesterday afternoon. But evidently he wasn't good at hiding his emotions, which were all over the place. "Yes, but I have news." He nodded toward the refrigerator. "Get started on your dough and I'll tell you while we work." He hadn't wanted it to sound like he was telling her what to do. But the urgency he felt pushed him.

She gazed at him for a few moments.

He tried to read her expression. What was she thinking?

Then she turned toward where the aprons hung on pegs on the wall. "Okay." Soon she was at her station next to him, rolling out her dough to shape it into loaves for the second rise. The fragrance of garlic and parmesan floated in the air. She glanced at him quizzically.

Now or never. He blurted, "I went to the community college yesterday and talked to a counselor."

Jess paused with the rolling pin in her hand. "Wow. What caused that?"

Chad drew in breath carefully, as if measuring each particle of oxygen. "You did."

"Me?" She sounded surprised.

"You told me—" He didn't want to reveal what had really motivated him. The effect of hearing that she was feeling more than friendship for him was too deep to be spoken. He substituted, "You told me to get some self-esteem, respect. It made me think that when I graduated high school, I never even went to the college to talk to the counselors there. Tom and Shirley wanted me to, but I thought, why bother? I didn't see myself as someone who could go to college."

Then Jess surprised him.

She swung toward him and put an elbow on each of his shoulders, keeping her doughy fingers away from his shirt. She kissed his cheek. "Oh, Chad, I'm so glad." She clasped her hands behind his head.

Feelings, sensations rioted inside him. He stood very still, holding it all in. He still had trouble believing that Jess had told him she was feeling... His mind stuttered on this memory. He couldn't doubt what Jess had said. She was as genuine as Tom and Shirley. He let himself revel in the memory as her elbows pressed against his ears. How could this simple contact move him so?

She kissed his cheek again and pulled away, looking flustered. Her cheeks pink, she began working her dough again. "What did the counselor say?"

Chad swallowed to wet his dry mouth. "He said I met the admission requirements since I graduated from high school with a reasonable rank. And he asked me what I was interested in studying."

"And?" Jess was shaping the dough into loaves, one by one. With business so good, she usually made two dozen loaves. People loved their rustic, hand-rolled appearance. He loved watching the deft movements of her small, delicate hands.

"I..." He hesitated, but this was Jess. He could trust her. "I said I might be interested in either law enforcement or culinary arts. I mean, I work for Tom, but repairing cars isn't really my thing, you know?"

"I get it. I know you enjoy working here more."

"You do?"

"Yeah, you whistle sometimes or hum while you work. I always liked that and it made me think you liked working with the dough, you know?"

He chuckled and shook his head. "I never realized that."

"I did." And then she looked at him. "But going into law enforcement might bring more respect."

Her words told him how much she understood the shadow

his father had cast over him. And he saw something new, wonderful in her gaze. He couldn't breathe.

Audra breezed in. "Good morning, staff!"

Her entrance broke their connection even as he reveled in the feeling of lightness, of joy that this brief conversation with Jess had ignited. The now too-familiar horrible dread descended over him—a dark blanket of worry and... His dad had been gone for six days now. Was there any hope? *Will I ever see him again...alive?*

<hr />

THAT AFTERNOON JESSIE had offered to clean the kitchen for Shirley and get supper into the slow cooker. The house was silent. She wondered where Dick and Florence were but maybe they were merely napping. She heard the front door open. Neighbors often opened the door and called for Shirley, announcing who they were.

But she heard the rumble of Dick's voice. "You're doing really well on those crutches, Flo."

A long, heavy sigh. "I'd rather pitch them into the lake."

Dick chuckled.

"But it was good sitting on the front porch," Florence said. "I wish I didn't get so tired so quick."

"You'll get better. It takes energy to heal."

"I know. I wish we'd appreciated how good we felt when we were young. I could do anything—"

"And you usually did." Dick's tone teased.

Jessie had heard this complaint of old age from other seniors. She guessed they forgot how uncertain being young was, how you made a choice and then regretted it. She stopped that line of thought. Wallowing in past mistakes was not of God. The pastor had said so in a recent sermon. It had hit home with her.

Chad came to mind. Thoughts of him came more and more often and she didn't resist them. Such a feeling swept through her, a drawing, a pulling toward him, even though he wasn't here. His telling her about visiting the community college lifted something inside her, a new realization. *I've just been marking time, making bread and working with Audra doing pizzas.* A new strength bubbled up inside. If Chad could go to college, why couldn't she go too?

"When will you move home, Dick?" Florence asked.

"I don't know if I will." Dick sounded down.

"What do you mean?"

"I can be honest with you, Flo. When I took Doyle in, I had two reasons. One was to give him one more chance to turn his life around."

Florence made a negative sound.

"You didn't lose a son in his twenties, Flo," Dick said in a quiet, sad voice. "My only son. I said to myself, if Ted had gotten off on the wrong foot, I'd have liked someone to help him."

"Sure, Dick. I get it." Florence sounded chastened, sympathetic.

"And the other reason"—Dick's voice became more brisk —"was because I realized I couldn't live out on my land alone any longer. Doyle is just in his early fifties and he was able to snowplow the drive and take me into town in bad weather. Shop, you know."

"I know. That's why I started paying to eat here. I don't need to shop for much. I just have toast or cereal for breakfast. I go to the congregate lunch most days and then I'm at Shirley's for supper. It's better."

"I know. If Doyle doesn't come back, I'll have to rent something in town."

"I got room at my place." Florence's voice sounded gruff.

"People will talk," Dick kidded her in a mock shocked tone.

"Let 'em. We been friends our whole life. I'm not lookin' for a man."

"You had plenty chasing you when we were in high school."

Florence chuckled. "I did. It's a nice memory. But I'm going to move downstairs. Shirley's convinced me. You could have the whole second floor. And do the meals like I do. Shirley even does my wash too. It's good."

There came a pause. "You're a good friend, Flo. And I'm grateful for your offer. Before Doyle moved in, I'd been alone for so many years. Miriam died too young—"

"I know what you mean. She was too young. My man was older than me. That didn't bother me till...you know."

"Yes, I know." He cleared his throat as if it had gotten thick with emotion. "And if Doyle doesn't come back..."

"I know," Florence said gruffly. "This has been awful, and I don't even like the man."

Their conversation paused again.

The silence went on long enough to worry Jessie. She crept to the doorway and down the hall. She glanced toward the two sitting in what Shirley persisted in calling the parlor. They were holding hands and had leaned toward each other, their foreheads touching. Jessie froze in place, uncomfortable intruding on this private moment.

"Let's get the cards out and play rummy a while. I don't feel like watching TV," Dick said after a few moments, sounding gruff and releasing Florence's hand.

"A penny a point?" Florence teased.

"Yeah, we're high rollers." They both chuckled.

Glad to hear Dick's tone lighten, Jessie crept back to the kitchen, pondering the sweet hand-holding and thought of how she now reached for Chad. Did love have an age limit? Or was this just two old friends comforting each other?

Jessie then wondered about the older woman's offer. It

made sense. Florence was encouraging Dick to look forward. And that's what Jessie needed to do for Chad. He must go forward—whether his father came back or not. Chad was worthy of respect and it was time he claimed it for himself.

———

NIGHT HAD COME AGAIN. As Doyle had anticipated, his captors returned in the dark. The sound of a motor, doors opening and shutting. They were coming. His heartbeat zoomed.

What would happen tonight? What would they do when they finally believed that he didn't have the information they wanted? Or would they ever believe the truth? He combed his mind for anything he could give them, any way he could survive this.

A very real fear that they might kill him or just leave him here to die reared up in his throat, nearly gagging him. *Oh, God, please help. Help.*

The door burst open, banged against the wall. "We're back."

"I'll do the talking." That same cool voice that somehow sounded familiar came from the darkness outside the door. "Get him."

The two men rushed him and before he knew what they were doing, he was sitting in a hard chair with his hands and feet tied to it. He knew what that meant. They were going to try to beat what they wanted out of him. He couldn't see their faces in the scant moonlight.

He drew in a deep breath of warm air. "I've told you, Getz didn't tell me anything. I can't tell you what I don't know. Do you think I've enjoyed this shed getaway?"

Silence.

A sound of amusement from outside. "I see your point."

"If I knew anything, would I have sat on it for three years?" Doyle continued. "I mean, I'm as poor as dirt. I barely keep my old pickup running. The only reason I got a place to live and something to eat is because I help out my uncle…" Mentioning his uncle cost him. Was Uncle Dick okay? "That's my life."

A long silence.

"You think this is about money?" the voice asked.

"It's about something of value," Doyle said, keeping his voice steady, trying not to show how he quaked inside. "Or why bother?"

Another longer silence.

"So," one of the big brutes near him asked, "can we rough him up? Or what?"

"Don't break anything or hurt his head. We need him to think. Talk. Last chance, Doyle."

"I got nothing," Doyle replied, trying to relax his muscles. Tightening them would only make it more painful.

He tried and failed.

One of them landed a blow to his chest. Doyle rocked with the impact. The other kicked his shins repeatedly with a pointed-toe boot. Doyle tried to remain loose but each blow caused a tightening he couldn't stop. He began gulping air.

"Okay, that's enough," the voice outside said. "Keski, you still got nothing for us?"

For a moment Doyle was tempted to make something up, but that would only make things worse. The pain of the beating rolled through him, weakening him. He slumped. "If I had anything," he forced out, "I'd tell you." He swallowed down terror. *Will they kill me now? Or just leave me here tied up to die slowly?*

Chapter 11

The long silence weakened Doyle more. The warm night air gathered around him, still, unmoving, almost taking his breath. The two who had taken pleasure in "roughing him up" waited near the open door, shifting on their feet, restless. The tension from their lingering menace wrapped around him as thick as the warm night air, sucking more of his strength away.

The voice from outside spoke at last, "Okay. I think I've thought of a way to make this worth all our time and trouble."

"Huh?" one of the men at the door turned toward the voice.

"Yes, I think this could still turn out to our advantage." The voice sounded self-satisfied. "Untie him. Leave the water and a bar. We'll be back, Keski."

"What are you going to do?" Doyle wasn't sure he wanted to know.

No reply came.

The men untied him and pushed him off the chair to the hard floor. The impact jarred him. They carried the chair away, and he could hear them set things inside.

"What are you going to do?" Doyle repeated, sounding as helpless as he felt.

The voice chuckled and the two men left, slamming, then locking the door behind them.

Doyle lay there curled up like a baby and as weak as a newborn. Bereft of hope. They believed he didn't have the information they had wanted from Getz. Or did they?

Oh, God, help. I'm sorry for all the crap I've done and sorry about everything I should have done but didn't do. I'm so scared... He was powerless in this situation. As powerless as he had felt for most of his days when the thirst for alcohol had ruled and ruined his life. Now he could only moan.

⬜

JULY 17TH

Chad led Jess into the trout stream where they had been fishing that horrible day exactly one week ago when everything had turned crazy. Craving being alone with her, he'd invited her to return here with him on a rare afternoon off. No pizzas at Audra's on Mondays and Tuesdays. The day couldn't have been more perfect with a clear blue sky, puffy white clouds, and a gentle breeze. The unusual heat and humidity had been pushed eastward with an atmospheric high controlling their weather.

"What do you think?" he asked Jess. "Will we have any luck?" His voice sounded shaky in his own ears. Did she hear it too? Was it because of the memory of being here a week ago? Or was it because he and Jess were totally alone here?

Jess gazed skyward to the blue above the tall, silent surrounding trees. "I don't know, but it's a lovely day. I'm glad you invited me." She turned her gaze on him.

What he saw in her expression caught around his heart. *Oh, Lord, she's so...* He couldn't find words to describe how special this woman was to him. *Why didn't I ever realize this before?* He tamped down his emotions that threatened to run away with him. With her history, Jess would not like a sudden rush. Two years ago, Tom had explained everything to Chad about what had happened to Jess. He must tread lightly. "I'll move downstream a bit." He motioned and was glad his voice sounded normal again.

"Okay."

Soon they were fishing, but something new, something between them, was different than all the other times they had come here to catch a few trout for supper.

Then it happened. He felt the fly catch his sleeve, the hook barely grazing his upper arm. He turned to Jess, who cocked her head to one side. "Oops. Here, let me untangle it. I don't want to rip your sleeve." She waded over to him, sloshing through the gentle current.

He analyzed her tone. Was it his imagination? Or didn't she sound very apologetic about hooking him?

Within moments she appeared beside him. As she bent her head and started carefully extricating the lure from his shirt, her hat brim touched his nose.

Having her so near yet not letting how it affected him show was torture. He could smell the scent of something like strawberries—maybe her shampoo? He drew in a deep breath of it.

She managed to unhook the lure. She looked up. "You do have a tiny rip. Sorry."

Her nose was inches from his. He moved his attention down to her lips, free of any lipstick but naturally lightly pink. He closed his eyes to keep himself under control. They'd just come here to fish as they had so many times before. Nothing more.

JESSIE RECOGNIZED that Chad was reacting to her nearness. This thrilled her. *He's feeling this too.* The thought of hooking his sleeve had flashed in her mind and she hadn't let herself quell it. That she'd gotten him with one cast astounded her. She'd never done anything that precise before. Then her feet told her to move one step forward and again she didn't argue. Her free hand lifted to his cheek. She found herself looking up into Chad's dark eyes. His name whooshed out with her breath. "Chad."

"Jess," he responded.

She smiled at his name for her. Her parents called her Jessica. Everyone else called her Jessie. Everyone except Chad. She rested her head on his tan fishing shirt and heard the thumping of his heart. Hers was behaving the same way. "Chad," she murmured, "you can put your arms around me. I want you to."

He put his rod down and obeyed. Then, pushing her hat back, he rested his cheek on top of her head.

The experience of being fully held by Chad filled her in a way she'd never experienced. She felt perfectly safe. Perfectly content. Until…she wanted more. She turned up her chin, stood on tiptoe with the brook rippling around her ankles. She halted with her lips just below his. "Lean down, Chad," she murmured. And waited.

Then Chad's phone in his chest pocket rang, startling them both. Jessie stepped back, a little unsteady, so she held on to Chad's upper arm. He pulled out his phone and said, "It's Harding." He tapped the phone to put it on speaker.

The sheriff? Concern clutched Jessie. Did he have news?

CHAD TRIED to concentrate on what the sheriff was saying. But what had almost happened between him and Jess distracted him. The sheriff's words jumbled in his ears. "Sorry, Sheriff, would you repeat that?"

"There has been a development in the case of your father's disappearance. Can you come down to my office?"

The news shot through Chad, igniting a mixture of relief and fear. "Sure. Now?"

"Now if you can."

"I'll come right over." He tapped his phone and stared at it. And then lifted his eyes to Jess.

"What do you think has happened?" Jess asked him.

"No idea." He pressed his lips together, holding back the turmoil that had been building up inside over the past seven days.

"Do you want me to come with you?"

He avoided answering her. "First, let's stop at Uncle Dick's like we planned. Want to make sure everything is okay before we head to the sheriff's office."

She nodded solemnly.

He had intended on stopping on their way here, but he didn't really want to go to Uncle Dick's empty house where so much bad had happened. But he'd promised his great uncle he'd check on things. The old house would be silent and foreboding. *Where are you, Dad? Are you still alive?*

Jess suddenly wrapped her arms around him. "Your dad's in God's hands. Whatever happens, we'll get through it."

He put one arm around her and buried his face in her hair once more. Finally, he straightened. "I guess the trout will have to wait until we come here again." It was a poor attempt at humor.

Yet Jess grinned up at him. "Right? I'm sure they were eager to dance on our jigs. But that's life." She shrugged.

He released her. "Let's go."

The visit to Uncle Dick's took only a few minutes. Everything was as he and Jess had left it when they'd gone to straighten things up before Uncle Dick had been expected to come home. That seemed weeks, not days, ago.

Then without a word between them, Chad drove them to the sheriff's office. He parked in front of the building, old but solid red brick. As they walked toward the door, Jess slipped her hand in his and he was grateful. He opened the door for her. After a few words to the receptionist, they entered Harding's office.

The sheriff rose and waved them to the chairs in front of his desk. "Thanks for coming right in." If the sheriff noticed him holding hands with Jess, he didn't show it.

Chad managed to nod, his mouth as dry as cotton balls.

"I won't draw this out." Harding picked up a paper from his desktop. "The crime lab rushed the DNA from your uncle's place since this was a probable kidnapping. We actually found some sweat to send them." He looked up. "It was a hot day, and sweat sprays if you're moving around, especially if you're fighting."

Chad slowly drew in a breath, steeling himself for what might be coming.

"What did they find?" Jess asked for him as if sensing he was having trouble making himself ask questions that might have answers he didn't want to hear.

"We were able to match one profile to someone other than your father or uncle, Chad."

"Okay," he muttered.

"We have the person in the system. In fact, he served time in the same prison your father did."

Chad sat up straighter. "Did he know my dad?"

"He might have, but they weren't in close proximity. Different cell blocks. But he's only been out for a couple of months." The sheriff gazed at them.

"So how is this going to help us find my dad?" Chad asked.

"I don't know. I'm going to talk to the prison warden, the

arresting officer, and detective on the guy's case, and anyone else that I think might know more about him. Find out who he knows. What he's capable of. It's our first real lead but…" He sucked in a deep breath. "I don't know yet why he would be involved in the disappearance of or perhaps kidnapping your father. But it's something real that I can follow up on."

Chad nodded, not knowing what to think, what to say.

"Do you have any questions for me?" Harding asked.

Chad couldn't think. His thoughts were scrambled eggs.

"Carter," Jess said, "we appreciate all you're doing on this. I know it's your job, but how long will this go on? I mean it's been a week…"

Jess had put his worst fear into words. How long would the kidnappers keep his dad alive? And why had they taken him?

"I don't know, Jessie. This is an odd kidnapping or whatever it is. We still can't find any motive for Doyle's being taken. I contacted the warden about his prison record. But got nothing. Doyle more or less didn't say anything to anyone while he was there. He kept to himself. And tried to avoid trouble." Harding lifted his hands and his shoulders in an expressive shrug. "I wish I had more to go on. But this is a lead, and I'll follow it wherever it takes me. And hope that it pans out."

"Thanks, Carter," Jess said, taking Chad's hand and rising.

Chad muttered his thanks too and gripped Jess's hand. Holding hands with her had become natural now. He needed a hand to hold. Harding's news didn't seem like it would lead anywhere, really. And a week had gone by. Chad felt sucked dry, empty, flimsy.

He kept her hand in his till he opened the pickup door for her.

She hoisted herself up and sat. From the high seat, she looked down at him. "Take me back to the stream."

He couldn't think why she wanted to go there. He was in no mood to fish now. But he shrugged. Soon he drove up the rough gravel road to their favorite angling spot and parked right where he had earlier.

Without a word, Jess got out and walked toward the gently rippling water.

He got out and followed her. When he stood beside her, she turned and embraced him.

The warmth and feel of her took his breath away. His arms went around her. He waited for her to say something.

But she merely rested her head against his shirt.

He waited. But the longing to finish what they'd started before Harding had called moved him to tuck her closer.

Finally, she took a deep breath and pushed back from him. "We started something here today. Shall we complete it now?"

He couldn't form words so he nodded.

Standing on tiptoe, she kissed him. Something warm and electric seemed to flow through him and he returned her kiss. "Jess," he whispered against her lips, "you make me feel..." He couldn't find the words he needed. Were there words wonderful enough to express how he felt?

"I know," she whispered. Then she moved backward slightly. "I've wanted to kiss you for days. But...all this with your dad and how busy we are and never alone..." She shrugged.

He nodded slowly, but her kiss had given him strength to face this. "Something is going to give. Something. It can't go on like this."

But it could. He knew of people whose loved ones disappeared and years later were still missing. Even in this beautiful place, evil could twist lives. *Dear God, help the sheriff find out something that will lead us to my dad.*

Chapter 12

July 18th

The trio who'd kidnapped Doyle were back the very next night. He had never been in as bad a shape as he was now, not in all his alcoholic days. He ached all over from sleeping on the hard floor. He stank of his own sweat. He was thirsty in a way he hadn't ever been. The jug of water they'd left last night was nearly gone. The three energy bars over the days had kept him alive but he didn't feel like he could go on like this much longer. Despair hung around his neck like a heavy chain ready to tighten and choke him.

The now too familiar routine started—the sound of the vehicle arriving, doors slamming, the shed door slapping open and then the two big guys filling the doorway. Doyle waited for the voice to speak from the darkness. What would it say tonight? Did they still think he had information or had they really moved on? Wordless prayers bubbled up inside him. He'd often felt hopeless, but now he was flat broke of hope and strength. He didn't even try to sit up to face them.

"Well," the familiar voice began, "we're back and we've got a plan. You must be worth something to someone, right? So if they'll pay to get you back, we'll get something for all our time and trouble."

They thought they deserved payment for what they'd put him through? Unbelievable. "I think," Doyle replied, hearing how faint his voice was, "you ought to be paying me."

The voice laughed. "It doesn't work that way, Keski. Now are you worth something to someone?"

The image of Chad came to Doyle's mind. The thought of putting his son, his good son, into this man's hands was unthinkable.

"Come on, Keski," the voice mocked. "We know you have a son."

"We heard about him on the radio," one of the hulking figures added.

"Shut it," the unseen voice snapped.

The two by the door shifted.

Doyle felt their agitation. They weren't the patient kind. He remembered how eager they'd been to rough him up, and his gut tensed.

"What about him?" Doyle spoke with caution.

"He got any money?" One of the two by the door spoke up again.

This was not a good sign. The voice had commanded these two until now, but the muscle was getting antsy.

"I said, shut it," the voice insisted. "You're going to mess this up if you don't let me take care of things. You want any money out of this or not?"

There was a brief silence. "Okay," one of the men replied. "But get it moving."

The two figures again folded their arms and leaned back against the wall. "Okay," one replied. Inwardly Doyle agreed with this.

"My son works two part-time jobs. He's not got much." The truth was easy and what might discourage them.

"How much do you think he'd give to get you back?" the voice asked.

Doyle resisted this idea. Chad was always polite to him. But they never really acted like father and son. "I don't know."

"What's his phone number?" the voice said, finally getting to the point.

"You're going to ask him for money?"

"What do you think?" one of the two by the door growled. "This hasn't been fun for us either, hanging around—"

"Shut it. Or I'll make you wish you had," the voice commanded. "And you know what I can do."

Silence.

Then the voice asked, "Do you need to be persuaded, Keski?"

Doyle drew in a breath. He didn't want to give them Chad's number. But the thought of being beaten in the nearly dead condition he was in triggered survival panic, flapping inside him.

"You know if you don't give us his number, we'll just go and grab him too."

That threat struck home. Doyle recited the number.

"Okay," the voice said, "that was smart. This way we can just call him and set up a drop. He won't have to see us, and we won't have to grab him. If he follows instructions, it'll go easy."

"Then you'll let me go?" Doyle heard the panic in his own voice.

"Yeah, your kid comes through, you'll be free and we'll be gone."

Doyle wanted to say more but he found he didn't have the strength.

Once again the two at the door went through their ritual of leaving water and an energy bar and left.

Doyle felt himself give in to despair but he was so dry that very few tears wet his cheeks. *God, take care of my boy. Don't let anything bad happen to him. Just take care of him. Please.*

MOONLIGHT ADDED a sheen to the houses along the alley. After finishing the pizza trade and clean-up at Audra's, Chad walked beside Jess. Their walk home was later than usual. Audra had ended up with too many orders right at the end and she had asked them to stay late. Thinking of the cost of school coming up, Chad had agreed and so had Jess. He had some savings, a few thousand dollars. If he could only decide which direction to go in—law enforcement or culinary arts, two completely different jobs. But that was the least of his worries now.

The alley was silent except for King, who always seemed to hear them coming and woofed to hurry them along. They had gotten into the habit of stopping to pet him and slip him a treat on their way home. Their fear of him was only a memory. His owner rarely came outside when he heard his dog. But tonight they saw he was changing a lightbulb on his back porch. He waved and they waved back then moved on.

The moonlight even shone on the rough asphalt beneath their feet. So quiet, so beautiful a night, while Chad felt ripped up inside between joy and worry. Walking beside Jess, his Jess, holding hands, lifted him in a way he'd never known. Yet worry about his father dragged at him as if a noose had wrapped around his neck and was relentlessly cutting off his air.

As though she sensed his mood, Jess drew closer and put an arm around his waist. Her freely given comfort nearly broke his resolve not to show how awful he felt. After all, she already knew. She knew the sheriff still had no firm idea what had happened. She led him to their bench. Another dog in a nearby yard finally stopped woofing.

Chad collapsed onto the bench and lowered his head, his elbows on his thighs, his hands hanging down loose. Broken.

Jess rested her hand on his back, murmuring to him. "God knows where your dad is. This lead to the guy who broke into your uncle's house might give us some information."

He gritted his teeth, wanting to snap at her. Instead he muttered, "I'm tired of waiting and worrying. I'm tired. Period."

"I know you're tired. I'm tired too, but we have to have faith."

Again he nearly snarled at her. Evidently, he didn't have enough faith. Did other people in this kind of situation just sit back, relax, and trust God? How did a guy do that?

"I was so tired two years ago of being the girl everyone talked about." She withdrew her hand. "I just wanted to remember who I was. I got tired and angry too."

He glanced toward her, sitting up straighter. "You did?"

"Yes. You weren't there on that Easter Sunday at Audra's mom's house when I had a meltdown. But I was upset most of those days. I felt...helpless."

Chad drew in a breath and leaned back against the wall behind the bench. "I'm exhausted. And worried and helpless."

Jess moved closer to him and rested her head on his shoulder. "I know," she murmured. Footsteps on the street behind them echoed in the silence.

He claimed one of her hands. Her presence comforted him. And he was finally able to put his worst fear into words. "What if we never find him?"

Jess wrapped both arms around his shoulders, her head still resting on him.

Chad opened his mouth to say something but his phone rang. He slid it out of his pocket. He didn't recognize the number. He nearly blocked it but then he felt the urge to answer. "What?" he snapped.

A strange voice chuckled. "Touchy, are we? This Chad Keski?"

"Why do you ask?"

"'Cause we got your dad. Do you want him back?"

Chad understood the words but couldn't quite believe them. "My dad?"

"Yeah, we got him. Do you want him bad enough to pay to get him back?"

Chad sat bolt upright. "How do I know you've got my dad? This case has been on the radio—"

"Here, Keski, say something to your kid," the stranger ordered.

"Chad…" A voice barely above a whisper came over the phone. "It's me, buddy."

The use of the nickname his dad had called him when he was a very little boy—before his mom had died and everything had fallen apart—hit him between the eyes. "Dad!" Chad's hand shook. "Dad, are you okay?"

"He's alive," the stranger replied. "Now here's the deal. No cops. We want five thousand dollars—"

Chad had trouble believing what he was hearing. "I don't have five thousand—"

There came a long pause. "We've wasted enough time already. So what have you got?"

"A little over three."

"Then get three thousand out in cash—unmarked. I'll call you tomorrow night to arrange a drop. No cops. Follow orders and you'll have your dear dad back tomorrow night—just a little worse for wear. Remember, no cops."

"I'm sorry, Chad." He heard his father's voice in the background and the stranger hung up.

His thoughts jumbled in his head. Shock and fear ricocheted through his mind and body. He realized that Jess was shaking his shoulder.

"Chad, what is it? Who was that?" She shook him harder. "Was it your dad?"

His mind scrambled wildly. Should he tell her?

"Chad, if you don't tell me right now, I'm going to go get Shirley and Tom—"

"No!" He bent his head, suddenly dizzy. "Give me a minute to catch my breath."

This quieted Jess. She leaned so close he could feel her breath on his cheek. Clouds moved over the moon and cut the light over them.

Chad felt his heart pounding and his breath panting as if he'd just sprinted. He did not want this…this thing with his dad to touch Jess. He went over in his mind what he'd just heard. What he'd just said he'd do. It didn't feel real.

"Chad, I want to know why you told someone you didn't have five thousand." Jess gripped his sleeve and shook it. "Was that dollars? Is it a ransom demand?"

He didn't want to answer her, but what choice did he have? "Yes, someone wants three thousand dollars for my dad."

———

THIS WAS EXACTLY what Jessie had guessed but hearing it confirmed slapped her in the face. The strength left her. She collapsed back against the wall behind them. All the movies she'd seen with ransom drops and the danger… She gulped air. "Oh, no."

"I didn't want to tell you," Chad said, sounding stressed. Somewhere nearby a door slammed.

She forced her hand to slide down his blue-jeaned thigh to his hand and took it into hers. "You couldn't hide it. I heard what you said." Her voice wobbled. She recalled watching scenes like this on TV, but never did she think she'd live one.

"Now tell me exactly what they said as best as you can remember." She gripped his hand tighter.

"They'll call tomorrow and tell me where to bring the cash. I bring the cash. They give me my dad. And no cops. I'm not supposed to—"

"Well of course they'd say that," she objected. "They don't want to be caught."

Chad turned to look at her. "But what if I tell Harding and they screw up and my dad—"

"What if you don't tell him and they take the money and make sure to leave no witnesses?" The horrible thought of losing this good man whom she was just beginning to love crushed her breath. She swallowed to regain equilibrium. "Chad, you have to tell Carter and get his help. Think. Remember what these men did to your uncle Dick. And we know one of them is an ex-con. These aren't people you and I want to face alone—"

"You're not facing them," Chad growled fiercely. "I don't want you anywhere near them."

"Guess what? I don't want you anywhere near them either. These are dangerous people, Chad." She strangled his hand between both of hers, trying to send her point home.

"I know they're dangerous."

"Then call Carter now. He'll need all the time he can get to prepare." She leaned forward and pressed her cheek to his. "For me, Chad. Please. I couldn't bear it if anything happened to you." The clouds moved, revealing the moonlight again. Jessie stared into his eyes that glistened in the low light.

Still, Chad made no move to take out his cell phone.

She wasn't taking no for an answer. She would fight him over this. She gripped his shirt sleeve. "Call him."

Chapter 13

Chad heard more than the fierce words Jess spoke. He heard the caring...the love behind them. Some feeling, one that awoke him in a new way, swelled within him. How could he refuse Jess? And she was right. He did not want to face the kidnappers alone. But...what if something went wrong?

Jess leaned closer.

In the distance a loon called, sounding something like a hysterical woman, like his fear. Understanding that he must agree—what choice did he have?—he tapped Audra's number on his phone. "Hi, Audra, is your husband home?" His voice betrayed his uncertainty. He tapped another button and put the phone on speaker.

"Sure. Carter," Audra said, "Chad wants to talk to you."

Soon Harding's voice spoke. "Chad, what's wrong?"

Chad wasn't surprised that Harding would jump to the conclusion something was wrong. He heard the concern in the sheriff's voice. He tried to answer. Had to swallow to moisten his mouth. "I got a call...from the kidnappers." Jess moved closer to him. Her warmth comforted him.

"Go on," Harding said.

Clouds floated across the moon above the rooftops. "They want me to take out three thousand...well, they wanted five but I told them I only have three—"

"So you've received a ransom demand," Harding said, his voice encouraging. "If they aren't asking for more than what you have, that tells me they want to get this over with and don't want any more people involved."

Chad digested this.

"When's the drop, Chad?"

"Tomorrow night. They'll call me with instructions." As Chad said these words, he again felt as if he was running the last desperate feet to win a race. How could words drain a person?

"I'm glad you called. It was the right thing to do. I've handled this kind of thing before. And I do need time to get everything in place for your safety and your dad's. First, I want to let you know what I found out about the one ex-con we identified with DNA."

Another string of fear zipped up Chad's spine. "What did you find out?" A night bird flew overhead, creating a breeze.

"He's a low-level criminal, what they'd call 'muscle' on a TV crime show. He was serving time for nearly killing a man. The warden told me that he was arrested with another man implicated in the same incident and they both were released on parole just a few weeks ago."

"How does that help us?" Jess asked.

"Oh, hi Jessie," Harding said, sounding happy to hear her voice. "It helps us understand the kind of people we're dealing with. From what the warden and the arresting detective told me about both men, they aren't guys who would do this on their own. They take orders, not give them. There must be another person involved who planned this. The warden is looking into the other felons who were in prison at the same time as your dad and who might have known him or known of him. And might have known these two."

Chad went over all this in his mind. "It's a lot to take in," he admitted finally.

"I know, Chad," Harding said, "but since you've given me time to work out the details, it should go smoothly. And tomorrow night you should have your dad back."

"Good," Chad said, hoping the sheriff was right.

"First," Harding cautioned him, "don't tell anyone else about this. Audra and I and you and Jess must keep this close. We don't want any spectators to show up. Or people thinking they can help. This has to be done right."

"We get that," Jess said.

"But what about Tom and Shirley?" Chad asked, somehow feeling he could face this better if they knew.

"Tom and Shirley, yes, but no one else," Harding agreed. "Second, don't come to my office. I doubt they're watching you, but we don't want to take chances. I don't know if they know that you work in my kitchen," Harding said with a touch of humor, "but just go about your daily routine tomorrow."

"Okay," Chad said, trying to believe he was having this conversation. Again, distant laughter made this conversation feel even less real.

"When you get the call, let me know immediately so I can trigger my department's response. You should tell me where you are and what they want you to do. Don't worry. I trained for this and so have my officers. I've done a drop before—"

"Successfully?" Jess cut in.

"Yes. No one was hurt, and I apprehended the kidnappers." Harding sounded confident.

"Okay," Chad said and let out a long breath.

"One last thing. Does the number of the phone that the kidnapper used to call you show on your cell?"

"Yeah," Chad replied and reeled off the number.

"It's probably just a burner phone, but I'll check on that too. Hang tight, Chad. And pray."

"Thank you, Carter," Jess said.

Chad ended the call. Again clouds cloaked the moon. In the darkness Jess's scent came to him, something like strawberries.

"Well, tomorrow is going to be a memorable day," Jess said, evidently trying to sound positive.

Chad took a moment to put the mix of hollowness and adrenaline he was feeling into words. "I feel like I just jumped off a cliff."

"I jumped with you," Jess replied and leaned into his embrace.

Something he'd seen often ever since Shirley and Tom had married came to mind. "Jess," he said, taking her hands in his, "let's pray together. You know, like Shirley and Tom do."

She looked into his eyes and solemnly nodded.

Chad had never prayed out loud before, but as Jess bowed her head, he followed suit. He couldn't think of anything but what he really wanted, so he spoke the words that came to him. "God, I just want my dad back."

"Yes, Father, this has been awful. Please let this end well."

Chad thought over what he'd said and what Jess had said and added, "We're going to trust You and the sheriff. Amen."

Jess came fully into his arms again and he held her, drawing strength from her presence.

———

JULY 19TH

Jess had insisted on coming to Audra's early with Chad the next morning. He appreciated her support, yet couldn't help feeling that he should handle this himself. But one look at Jess's determined face in Shirley's kitchen warned him not to tell her she didn't need to go with him.

So now, here in this white and stainless steel kitchen, Jess stood near the sink across from him. He had just begun working with the yeasty-smelling sweet bread dough.

Audra and Harding entered the kitchen and Jess's hands froze up in her dough.

"It's convenient that you two come here every day," Harding said. He pulled a stool out from under the counter where Chad stood and sat down.

"Sheriff," Jess said, sounding worried.

Chad's stomach had been unsettled since last night's kidnapper's call. Now it rolled, churned. "Hi," he managed to reply.

Harding considered him. Looked as if he wanted to say something. Shook his head and glanced down at his phone. "I'm going to take you through what I've set up and then we'll go over what you need to do...and not do."

Audra gently nudged Chad toward the sink. "Wash your hands and sit down with Carter. You need to keep your mind on this. I'll work the dough while you listen."

Chad nodded, feeling a vacuum in his brain. He was hearing the words, sort of understood them, but he felt disconnected somehow. Still, he washed his hands. Jess hadn't moved since the sheriff and Audra had entered. Now she washed her hands and began filling the pot with water for coffee.

"First of all, Chad," Harding began, "you will look like you're alone but you won't be. We have an agreement with a used car dealer in Ashford. We rent older cars and pickups when we're tailing someone."

"Tailing me?" Chad heard the squeak in his voice and cleared his throat.

"Yes, we're not letting you do this alone—"

"But they said no cops—"

"And they will see no cops. Our first priority is to get your dad back safely, but we also want to apprehend the people who have done this to your great uncle and your father. They shouldn't get away with this. And go on to hurt others."

Jess finished filling the pot with water and began measuring coffee grounds into the basket.

"But we'll get Dad first, right?" Chad couldn't stop the quaver inside him.

"Right." Harding nodded once without hesitation. "Your father's and your safety will be our first priority. But I don't want to let these people get away with this, especially not in my county." The sheriff's last few words came out fierce.

This reassured Chad, but his stomach still felt touchy, as if he'd eaten something that was going to come back up.

The sheriff went on to detail the GPS trackers that they would plant in Chad's truck, cell phone, and clothing. "We'll be able to track wherever you are."

"Won't they check for them?" Chad asked, thinking again of TV shows he'd seen about ransom drops.

Jess finished prepping the coffee and sat down on the stool next to Chad. Her nearness bolstered him.

"I'm sure they will, but we'll have more than one on you, and I'm going to have one sewn into your clothing. We'll let them find the one—but not make it too easy. We don't want them to get suspicious." He patted Chad's shoulder. "I've sent out a request for support, and we'll have more than our usual force out in various used vehicles. You won't be alone, Chad. But we'll make it look like you are."

Chad found he couldn't speak. He nodded and, sealing the deal, held out his hand.

Harding shook it. "We'll get your dad back."

"What should we do today?" Jess asked. "Besides getting the money out."

"Except for that, just go through your normal routine as

best you can. We don't know who they are. And it's tourist season, so we have a lot of strangers in town. They won't stick out. Chad, it's all right to look worried, but as much as possible just do your normal day."

Chad nodded like a ventriloquist's hand was up the back of his head.

Harding rose. "I've got things to do. Now here's my best advice. Just do what the kidnappers tell you to do and leave the rest to us."

"I think we should pray about this," Jess said, reaching for Chad's hand.

Her touch rippled through him, exciting but also comforting. He tugged her closer. "Sheriff?"

Harding rose and moved close to his wife, whose hands remained deep in dough. "Father, this is all in Your hands. Help me as I coordinate and direct the push to get Doyle safely home. Our trust is in You alone. Amen." Harding looked up and smiled again. "I don't usually pray with those who come to me for help. I wish more asked." He kissed his wife's cheek, squeezed Chad's shoulder, and left the room.

"Chad," Audra said, "you don't need to work this morning if you don't feel like it."

"I think I need to keep busy." Chad heard his inner trembling come out in his voice.

Jess moved closer to him. "We'll get through this."

Chad nodded, unable to move his wooden lips. One way or another this would all end today. Fear squeezed inside him. *God, I do trust You, but...*

━━━

THIS DAY HAD BEEN the longest day in Chad's life. Now just after dark, the wall clock in Shirley's kitchen read 10:42. Jess would come home soon. She'd worked the pizza trade with

Audra that was busier than ever and was going to set up her morning bread dough and then come home. Chad wished he'd been able to stay with her, but the sheriff wanted him here. The plans for following him to the drop were all set.

Not in on what was going on tonight, Uncle Dick and Florence were in the living room watching the loud TV. Chad sat at the kitchen table, Tom and Shirley opposite him. The ceiling fan kept the air moving. Soon the lake breeze would begin to cool them. He was trying to appear normal. He hadn't felt this much tension since before he'd come to live with Shirley when he was nearly in high school. After his mother died, he had felt like he was living in a pressure cooker. His father's frequent drunken rages had terrified him. But after living with Shirley for years, those memories had faded. He'd been able to count on the fact that in her house he didn't have anything to fear.

Now Shirley reached over and pressed her hand on his in silent support. He read the concern and love in her gaze. It almost brought tears to his eyes. The reason he'd begun believing in God had started with Shirley loving him no matter how badly he behaved. In thanks for that, he squeezed her hand.

His phone rang. He felt the unseen ripple of fear in himself and around him. He tapped his phone to speaker, preparing himself for whatever came. "Hello."

"Okay, kid," the same voice as in the previous call said. "Get in your truck and drive out of town on the county road going east. Keep your phone close. Just keep on that road and wait for further instructions." *Click.*

Everyone at the table rose. Tom gazed at him. "We'll be praying non-stop, Chad. May God go with you."

Chad tried to speak, cleared his throat, and said, "I know that. I trust Him." He suddenly wished Jess were there so he could feel her in his arms, but she was better off far from this.

Before his courage could fail him, Chad headed out the door to his truck in the alley. The night sky glittered with stars and he could hear people laughing in the courtyard of a nearby bar. He was on the way to face kidnappers. *Oh, Father, help me, go with me, please.*

Chapter 14

July 19th

Chad drove down the familiar county road, heading west where fewer people lived. His already high tension level tried to leap higher but he kept praying for strength, keeping the fear at bay. He knew he wasn't up to facing this without backup. He trusted Harding to do his best. But God was the biggest backup he could call on. Still God didn't feel close right now. His fear shut everything else out. The minutes went on. He gripped the steering wheel as if trying to control the emotions jumbling inside him.

Finally, his phone rang. He cleared his throat and answered it. "Yeah?"

"You made good time." The voice said. "Ahead on your right is an old logging road. Pull into that far enough so no one can see you from the road. And park." *Click.*

They must have been watching for him. He glanced around but could see nothing but trees. The realization that they might be close hit him. Sweat drenched him. He followed the instructions. As his motor settled into being shut off, the truck engine ticked. Silence. He rolled down his window and waited. A few minutes passed. Where were they? His heart thumped against his breastbone.

Then he realized they were making him wait in order to make him more tense. He wouldn't let that happen. He drew in breath slowly and let it out, the way his counselor had taught him. He relaxed muscle groups and felt some tension ease. He would not let them manipulate him any more than he must in this situation.

Finally, he heard the brush that crowded against the old logging track rustling with movement. They were driving up behind him. He turned to look—

"Keep your eyes forward!" that same voice who'd called him commanded. "Get out of the truck. Shut the door and put your hands on the hood. And don't move! Or look back!" Car doors opened and slammed.

Goose bumps shot over Chad's skin as he obeyed. The truck hood was warm from the drive here.

"We're going to blindfold you. So stand still. If you don't see us, all the better for you." The voice radiated with menace.

Someone came up behind Chad and he had to force himself to stand still, keep looking down. Some kind of cloth was slipped over his eyes and tied very tightly behind his head.

"Turn around," the voice commanded.

Chad obeyed.

"Now, after listening on the radio, we know you're some kind of relation to the sheriff. So we're betting you told him— even though we told you not to. So my friend here is going to relieve you of your phone, then frisk you for any trackers or mics or anything. Don't move."

Chad again forced himself to keep breathing steadily, not let fear take over. But it wasn't easy to stand there and let himself be manhandled. His phone was pulled out of his pocket and he heard it hit the gravel of the rough road.

"Found a tracker," a different voice announced. The man

pulled at the back of Chad's waistband. Chad froze as the blade of a knife grazed his low back. The tracker tucked into his waistband was cut free.

"Keep looking," the voice commanded.

The rough hands again swept over Chad, up and down and into personal places. He fought to let it go on without revealing his revulsion, his outrage at being mauled.

The man found the tracker sewn into the hem of his cargo shorts. Chad heard the man snap open a knife. He nearly yanked Chad backward as he slashed the cloth, grazing the skin in the fold of Chad's left knee.

"Is that all?" the first speaker asked.

"Yeah," the mauler replied.

"You feel where the money is?"

"He's got a thick folded wad in his right cargo pocket."

"Pull it out—"

"Hey, where's my dad?" Chad objected, reaching down to protect the lower pocket.

"Chill," the voice he'd begun to sincerely dislike said. "We're taking you to your dad. But first we got to see if you brought the money."

The mauler unbuttoned the pocket and yanked out the envelope with all Chad's savings.

His instinct to resist soared to life. Yet Chad held himself in check. He was outnumbered and blindfolded and he'd come for one reason. "Where's my dad?"

"We're going to take you to him. We're going to leave your truck here since it probably has a tracker or two on it too. My friend is going to walk you to our car and put you in the trunk. We have a little ways to go to your dad. And don't take off that blindfold!"

Chad didn't want to get into any trunk, but what choice did he have?

The mauler grabbed his arm and hustled him several yards

over the uneven wild grass. Chad heard a trunk opening, and then the mauler half-lifted and shoved Chad into the trunk. The lid came down and within moments, the motor started. Chad felt around, feeling even blinder in this cave. But evidently they'd cleared out the trunk.

Again he tried to relax his muscles and not let himself concentrate on the darkness and motion and the fact that he was trapped. After all, they hadn't found the tracker hidden in his belt. He just had to hang in there and trust that Harding was doing his job. He repeated to himself, *I'm not alone.*

The road was rough and soon his stomach got queasy. How far did they have to go? Chad's prayers became a litany: *Get me through this. Let me get my dad back.*

Finally, the car stopped abruptly, throwing Chad against the trunk latch. The minutes had given him too much time to think and worry. Would he see his dad now? Or had they killed his dad and would now try to do away with him? A sick feeling sank from his stomach to his toes.

━━━

AS JESSIE STEPPED into the night and shut the kitchen's Dutch door behind her, she called over her shoulder, "See you tomorrow, Audra!" Earlier Shirley had called to tell her and Audra, who had still been cleaning up after the pizza trade, that Chad had gotten the call and left. *Oh, Father…*

She thought of where Chad might be now, what he might be facing. Her heart jumped and lurched in her chest. But while Chad was off meeting the kidnappers, she was supposed to act as naturally as possible. The alley seemed quieter than usual. She wished this could have been a full moon night, but a crescent or fingernail moon hung above her.

The bar and grill on the main street to her right was busy. When people went in and out, she could hear snatches of country music. *Oh, Lord, please be with Chad tonight. Bring him home safely—*

Someone plowed into her. She gasped. A meaty hand clamped over her mouth.

Not an accident!

Self-defense training snapped on. She resisted pulling away and collapsed against her assailant, throwing him off balance. He released his hold on her mouth and screamed, "Help! Fire! Help!"

He grabbed her again. Tried to cover her mouth. She choked out a scream again as black spots danced in her vision.

———

CHAD HEARD the trunk latch being turned and then fresh air flooded his face. He was yanked out of the trunk. As his feet were planted on the ground, he stumbled, off balance.

A strong hand clamped on his arm and half-dragged him forward.

"Where's my dad?" Chad demanded. "You've got the money. Where is he?"

"Go ahead, Keski, answer him," the voice ordered.

"Chad…I'm here."

The weakness of his father's voice propelled him forward.

But the strong arm clamped tighter. "You ain't goin' nowhere," the mauler growled.

"Bring him over here," the voice ordered.

Chad was dragged forward.

"Now we're just about done with you. But we've taken a necessary precaution. We think we got you disconnected from any way the law can find you quickly and easily. But we didn't want to take any chances."

What had they done? Chad froze.

"Yeah," the mauler agreed, "don't want to go back—"

"Shut it," the voice snapped.

"What are you talking about?" Chad asked, trying to sound calm. He was still trying to get any clues about these two and where he was. In the background, his father's ragged breathing distracted him and worried him. What had they done to him? How bad was he?

"That pretty little girl you walk home with at night from that bakery—"

Chad's anxiety went off like a Roman candle firework. "Jess!" Rage filled him, hot and wild. He lunged blindly forward.

The mauler grabbed him and shook him.

"She'll be all right," the snarky voice jeered. "He's not going to hurt her. Just keep her a while."

Chad drew in air. "I think you're bluffing," he said, but doubted his own words.

"We got that covered," the voice said. "She'll tell you herself."

Fear grabbing and twisting his nerves, Chad heard the man tapping in a number on his cell. And heard it ring and ring. And ring.

No one answered.

"What the…" the voice grumbled, sounding irritated.

He tapped again. The phone rang and rang and…

The voice cursed loud and long. "I'll kill that—"

Then chaos.

Sirens from every direction.

Surprised shouts from the mauler and the voice.

Chad wrenched the cloth off his eyes. In the faint moonlight, he glimpsed armed, helmeted cops bursting through the thick forest from all directions. Out of the corner of his eye, he saw the two strangers—the kidnappers—running to a car.

"Stop, police!" Harding's voice magnified by a bullhorn commanded.

The two kept running.

"Stop!" Harding commanded again. A huge spotlight snapped on, flooding the small clearing and nearly blinding Chad.

He didn't care if the kidnappers were caught. He only wanted to find his father. He tried to shield his eyes with his hand. "Dad? Dad? Talk so I can find you. Dad!"

"Chad," the weak voice replied. "Son."

Chad plunged toward the sound.

"Stop!" Harding commanded again.

In seconds Chad's eyes adjusted to the bright light. Hearing but not paying attention to the loud commotion going on behind him, he continued straight for his dad, who was lying on the ground. He looked like a pile of rags. Swamped with compassion, Chad reached him and dropped to his knees. "Dad, are you all right?"

"Son," Doyle said and then lost consciousness.

A few gunshots exploded. Chad bent over his father to protect him.

"Don't shoot!" a voice begged.

"Hands behind your heads!" Harding ordered.

Chad swung around. The two men he'd only heard or felt before were standing near a vehicle with their hands behind their heads. Officers were closing in on them.

"Take them into custody," Harding ordered. "Read them their rights."

Chad looked up and saw Harding heading his way. Chad sprang up. "They said they had Jess."

Harding jerked to a stop. "Jessie?"

"They called it insurance. But when they tried to call her, they got no answer. And see, there are only two here." He was scrambling to get the words out, make the sheriff understand. "I mean—there must be a third. You said there might be. They couldn't get him on the phone but he could still have grabbed her—"

Harding's cell rang. "What?" he barked into the phone.

Chad didn't like the way Harding's face deepened into a mix of anger and worry. Then his face cleared. "Okay. Good. We'll be bringing in the suspects soon. Now signal the ambulance." He looked down. "Keski definitely looks like he needs medical attention." He disconnected the call.

Chad looked at him, wanting to drag the information from him if it didn't come right now. "What happened? Is Jess all right?"

Harding squeezed his shoulder. "I don't have time to explain now. She's safe. I'll be back." The sheriff hustled toward the officers who'd circled the suspects.

An ambulance siren blared nearby and within moments rocked over the rutted track into sight.

"Over there!" Harding called and motioned.

Chad dropped to his knees again. "Help's here, Dad."

With sunken eyes, his dad looked up, blinking. "Sorry… Son. Uncle Dick?"

"It's not your fault, Dad. Uncle Dick's fine. And Jess is okay and you'll be okay." Chad's voice cracked on the final words. Before he could say more, paramedics swarmed around him and began treating his dad. He rose and stepped out of the way.

Harding broke away from the group of officers to Chad's left and returned to him. "They'll be behind bars within the hour."

"Where's Jess? What happened to her?"

"From the little I gleaned, the third member of this gang tried to grab her as she walked home."

"No!" Chad's hands fisted. *Jess, no.*

"Don't worry. She's fine. These people underestimated her

and your neighbors. Come on. I'll head to the hospital in Ashland—"

"I want to go to Jess first—"

"She'll be at the hospital too."

That stopped Chad. "Why, if she's okay?"

"Let's get going. Not talking. You'll see her and she'll explain everything to us. Get in the ambulance and go with your dad. I'll have someone drive your truck to the hospital. Go!"

Chapter 15

July 20th

Tired but keyed up by all that had happened to her and Chad, Jessie paced back and forth in front of the Emergency Room entrance. Outside, the dark of this early morning hour cloaked everything but what the taillights illuminated, giving an unnatural feeling to the already unnatural night. She'd been told that Chad and Doyle were on the way in the ambulance. Behind her, Shirley and Tom sat also waiting, holding hands. Waiting to see Chad in the flesh was worse than the few bruises she'd suffered tonight. She drew in a cleansing breath and let it out and continued praying.

Then she heard it, the siren in the distance! She stood to the side of the automatic doors, watching. The ambulance surged up to the entrance and halted. An EMT jumped out of the cab and hustled around. The rear doors swung wide and then…Chad climbed down.

Chad. Jessie held herself tightly in check as she watched the gurney being lowered from the back of the ambulance. She strained to get a good look at Chad's father, wrapped in blankets and strapped to the gurney. How bad was he?

Chad looked up, and in that instant all the feelings she had for him swelled like a fountain.

He left the gurney and ran to the automatic doors. He burst through.

Chad gathered her into his arms. "Jess, Jess."

She clung to him, then lifted her face to his.

His lips claimed hers with a fervor she could only answer with her own. He was safe. He'd come to her.

He drew her to one side, letting his father and the EMS crew enter and be met by the hospital staff. Then he released her but only slightly, keeping her beside him with an arm around her waist. "You're all right?"

"Don't worry about me. Chad, I was so worried about you."

He studied her. "What happened to you?"

She looked away, avoiding thoughts of the alley experience. She would tell him when this was all over, his dad taken care of. "I'll tell you later. What happened with the kidnappers? Did they get them?"

Chad studied her another moment and then said, "Yes. Everything went just as Harding said it would. But what happened to you?"

"It isn't important." The sudden spurt in her pulse belied this but she said a silent prayer of thanks. "Help came when I needed it—" Noise from around the gurney distracted Jessie.

And Chad's attention switched to his father.

"Go on," Jessie urged, seeing that he was torn. "I'm fine. You need to be with your father."

Chad hesitated.

"You need to be with your dad," Jessie insisted, pushing him. "We'll talk later. I'm fine. Really."

"Just a moment," Shirley spoke up from behind Jessie. "I need a hug too." Shirley held out her arms toward Chad.

He left Jessie and hugged Shirley and then Tom. Shirley

was wiping tears from her eyes. "I'm so grateful to God. He protected you."

After kissing Shirley's cheek, Chad gave Jessie another quick hug and then hurried to catch up with the entourage of doctors and nurses crowded around Doyle's gurney.

Shirley put an arm around Jessie's shoulder. "We need to get back home and try to get some sleep yet." She glanced at her wristwatch. "Dick and Florence will be waking early, as usual."

"I'll come with you," Jessie said. "I can't do anything here, and I'm really tired. I just needed to see Chad—"

"And he needed to see you," Tom said. "We'll leave a message for him that we've gone home and not to worry. He'll be fine."

Jessie hesitated. She wanted to stay here but Chad needed, wanted, to be with his father. Later he would come home to Shirley and Tom's and they would have time to talk. A full day's work, the tension of worrying about the drop, and then the shock of the attack. All this, plus her bumps and bruises, were dragging her down. She let out a long breath. "You're right. I'm beat. Chad must stay with his dad, and he'll come home and then we can talk."

Seeing Chad…kissing him had brought joy, but her adrenaline had vanished with the relief from it all. She walked between Shirley and Tom toward the automatic doors, praying for Chad's dad and thanking God for their safe rescue. And her own escape from harm.

⸺

"JESS, JESS," a voice whispered into her ear. She tried to brush it away.

"Jess, you can't get rid of me that easy," a familiar voice teased.

Chad! Her eyes flew open and she turned toward him where he knelt by her bed. "Chad—"

He interrupted her with a soft kiss on her lips.

She returned the kiss.

When it ended, he rose. "Shirley sent me up to get you for breakfast. Company's coming, and I want to hear what happened to you from you. Come on. Get up and get dressed."

"How's your dad?" she asked him as he turned toward the door.

"He'll be fine. Just starved and dehydrated. He'll get out of the hospital later today. Come on. I'm hungry! And nobody will tell me your story. They said I had to wait for you."

Jessie glanced at the clock and a shock hit her. "My alarm didn't go off. We're late to work—"

"Audra put up a closed sign this morning. She's downstairs too. Hurry."

Jessie climbed out of bed, hurriedly freshened up, and dressed in a fresh T-shirt and shorts. Company for breakfast? She could guess who that was. She hurried down the stairs, beckoned by the sound of many voices in the kitchen.

She stopped on the last step and centered herself. She'd be expected to tell Chad the story of what happened in the alley last night. Everyone was worrying about her, but they shouldn't. *I'm not afraid anymore.*

She stepped through the kitchen doorway and saw Dick and Florence sitting side by side as were Shirley and Tom. Audra and their neighbor Greg, with King at his side, crowded around the table too. Chad sat beside Greg, looking a bit confused by their presence. King immediately barked his welcome to Jessie. Seeing all those who were concerned about her, cared about her, gathered here in this familiar kitchen nearly brought tears to her eyes. She blinked them away so no one would misunderstand.

CHAD ROSE, his heart full of gratitude. Jess was here with him and his dad was in the hospital getting the care he needed. "Jess?" He pulled out the last vacant chair for her. She sat down and Shirley stood and quickly poured her a cup of coffee.

Chad enjoyed watching Jess add cream and one teaspoon of sugar as usual. Every little thing she did seemed precious to him. But he didn't like the bruise on her cheek he'd just noticed.

She took her first sip of coffee and swallowed.

Chad wanted her to begin her story right away but continued to wait, giving her space. What had happened to her last night? Had it brought back bad memories?

"Well, the suspense is killing me," Florence blurted. "Jessie, I know someone grabbed you last night in the alley. Tell us what happened. I want to hear it from you."

Greg cleared his throat and countered, "Well, I think I'll tell the story and let this girl eat some breakfast."

Shirley opened the oven and lifted out a plate of pancakes and sausages. She reached over and set it before Jess. "Go ahead and eat. We'll tell the story. You need your breakfast."

Jess chuckled and reached for the maple syrup. "Yes, Mom. And thanks, Greg, you tell it."

"Last night I was watching some nonsense television show," Greg began. "As usual, King was out in the backyard, waiting to greet Jessie and Chad on their way home and get his usual treat and pets. Then I heard someone yell, 'Help! Fire! Help!' I jumped up and ran. When I opened the back door, I saw King leap over the fence, barking like mad. I knew that bark. He was on duty. I grabbed my sidearm and headed for the alley too."

"Sidearm?" Chad questioned, shocked.

"Yeah, when I moved here, I decided not to tell anyone

that I retired from the Milwaukee Police Department along with King. He was my K-9 partner for the last eight years of my career. I waited till he was going to be retired and then I did too." Greg paused to look at Chad. "Your girl handled herself real well. That getting free enough to scream made all the difference. Well, by the time I reached the alley, King had the attacker by the forearm. He was holding on while the guy tried to beat him off, yelling and cursing."

"I'd gotten away," Jess said between bites. "King was terrifying. I was almost scared for the guy…almost."

"Don't waste any sympathy on him," Greg said. "He knew what he was up to, and it was no good from what the sheriff told me. Evidently, he stole a car and was supposed to grab Jessie and drive her to a pre-arranged spot where she could be found after a few hours' search. Those creeps who grabbed Chad's dad wanted to keep the law busy while they got away. Didn't work." Greg smiled and scratched King's ears. "You can still bring a suspect down easy, can't you, boy?"

Chad rolled all this around in his head, unhappy and feeling a bit guilty that he hadn't been there when Jess needed him. He bent down and said to King, "I owe you a prime sirloin steak, King, and you'll get it as soon as I get to the store."

King woofed just as if he understood.

Everyone around the table chuckled.

"Don't stop eating," Chad encouraged Jess. "You need a good breakfast after last night."

"So do you," she responded and then forked up a bite of pancake dripping with maple syrup.

Chad patted his stomach. "Already did that. You didn't think Shirley would let me go hungry, did you?" It felt good after the last ten days to speak of everyday things like eating breakfast. Still, the fact that the kidnappers had hurt Jess stung deep. He wished he could have slugged one of them.

"I'm really impressed," Greg said, "with your local sheriff and his department. He brought the operation off without a hitch. Well done."

"He's my husband," Audra said. "I'll let him know that you were happy with the way things went."

Greg lifted his coffee cup in a salute to her. King barked as if in agreement. Everyone around the table chuckled again.

"Chad," Jess asked, "how's your dad? Were you able to talk to him?"

"No, not really. He was too weak and they didn't want him excited. I just sat with him all night. And then came home for breakfast and to shower and change. I'm going back in a bit. I'm hoping we'll have time to talk. He's been through something awful. I'm concerned."

Both Jess and Shirley patted his arms.

Uncle Dick cleared his throat. "Flo and I have an announcement to make." He glanced at Florence who nodded, suddenly smiling broadly. "Flo and I have decided to get married soon, and I'll move into her house. We're both appreciative of your taking us in, Shirley and Tom, but we've decided we'd be better off together but still living next door to you. We expect to pay you, Shirley, for all you do for us just like Florence has, but we would like to stay in her home together if you'll continue to help us."

Chad wondered at this development. But now that he thought of it, hints of this romance had been evident.

Shirley glanced at Tom, who nodded. "Of course," Tom said. "We'll continue to help you two. You're neighbors and we're glad to be of service."

"We don't know how long we'll have together," Florence stated gruffly, "but we want to be happy here where we belong as long as God gives us."

Uncle Dick put an arm around her and squeezed. "This has been an awful ten days but something good has come from it. Flo and I have a lot of history. We both loved our spouses, but we've both been alone a long time."

"And I think that something good has come for more than just us, Dick," Florence said, casting a knowing glance at Jess and Chad. "We heard about that kiss in the emergency room. Don't scold Shirley. The two of us have been watching you for a while wondering when it'd dawn on you that you were perfect for each other."

Chad didn't know what to say to this. He felt himself blushing.

Jess rested a hand on his arm. "I think that's something Chad and I need to talk over. In private."

This announcement was greeted with knowing grins.

Feeling unsettled yet hopeful, Chad looked at the wall clock and then at Jess. "I need to go back to the hospital."

"I know," Jess agreed. "We don't need to talk today. We have time, all the time we need." Then she surprised him with a light kiss on the lips right there in front of everyone.

He blushed warmer. And tried not to mind the knowing grins getting broader. He petted King once more and then rose to return to Ashford Hospital. Everything had come right, except for the conversation he'd long wanted to have with his dad, the one where they at last made the peace he hoped for. He prayed he'd have the words he needed. And feel the forgiveness he knew would be right. So much emotion roiled to the surface. Bad memories tried to come, but he pushed them away. The past was dead and gone. He wouldn't let it spoil today, the day they'd admitted their feelings for one another to those who loved them.

At the last minute, he turned back, still wanting to stay. But Jess sent him a sweet smile filled with promise. She would be here waiting for him when he returned.

Chapter 16

July 20th

Getting his father out of the hospital in Ashford had been as time-consuming and tedious as Chad had expected. And his father had been silent all the way home to Uncle Dick's house. Chad had wrestled with flashes of memories he rarely thought of anymore, bad times when his father had taken out his drunken rages on him. These had been supplanted by images of Shirley and Tom's gentle but firm parenting. It was a battle. But Chad intended to win it today and finally connect with his father. Or give it his best effort.

Chad pulled up in front of the house and parked. He slid out but noticed that his father hung back. He walked around and opened the passenger door. "Do you need help, Dad?"

His father didn't reply but got out of the truck. He paused, looking at the house. "I thought Uncle Dick would be home."

"Oh, he's been staying at Shirley's. He didn't want to stay here alone." Chad chose not to mention Uncle Dick's injuries from the break-in that had started what they'd just gone through.

His dad stared at the house. "Is he all right?"

"Yes, he's fine now. Come on." Chad put an arm under his dad's elbow.

"Is he still staying in town?"

"Yes. Florence has also been staying at Shirley's. She fell and broke her ankle. I think Uncle Dick stayed to keep Florence company. And that led to something interesting." Chad let himself grin.

"With Florence?" His dad's surprise sounded in his question.

Chad got his dad moving. He let the question hang in the air as he unlocked the front door and ushered his dad inside.

"What about Florence?" his dad persisted.

Now Chad heard a kind of panicked edge to his dad's voice. "They're getting married."

His father took this as a physical blow and staggered.

Chad grabbed his arm and supported him to the sofa. "Sit down, Dad. I'll get you some water."

"Where will I go?" his dad asked.

"Well, I guess you'll stay here." Chad sat down beside him.

"Uncle Dick just keeps me here to help him out. And Florence hates my guts." His dad actually started to shake.

Chad grabbed his shoulders. "Dad, Uncle Dick had you come live with him because you're family, his only sister's only son. He's told me that more than once. You're family."

"I'm lousy family. Why do you even care? I was never a good father." His dad hung his head.

Chad saw the opening and took it. "You're right. After Mom died, you let me down." He paused, letting this sink in. "But that's in the past. I think it's time that we start being... connected again. Don't you?"

His dad looked up. "Connected?"

"You're my father. You couldn't be a good one when the drink had you. Shirley explained that to me. Dad, you can't go back and change the past. But why don't we stop keeping our distance? Don't you want that too?" This last sentence caught around Chad's lungs.

His dad looked away. "I don't deserve that—"

"It's not about deserving," Chad cut in. "You're my dad. I'm your son. You hold yourself apart from me. And I don't know how to…connect with you."

"Why would you want to have anything to do with me?" His dad appeared to fold into himself.

Chad thought of all Shirley and Tom had done for him, no matter how badly he acted. They had done it because of what God had done for them.

As if reading Chad's mind, his dad muttered, "Tom Robson has been more of a dad to you than I ever was." He hung his head and with his elbows on his thighs, his hands hung limply.

"You're right," Chad said, "but he isn't my blood, is he? You're my father." Chad emphasized the last word. "It hurts me that we don't connect. Dad, what happened to change you? Why did you finally stop drinking?"

His dad gripped his hands together between his knees.

Chad waited.

"When I was in prison, my cellmate died. I couldn't help him. I called the guard for help. But he was too late. Before he died my cellmate kept saying, 'I don't want to go to hell.' He repeated that over and over and before long it was like I was saying it. It scared me. I hadn't thought of hell or heaven for many years. Not since your mom died." Chad's dad hazarded a glance toward him. "Your mom was a Christian. She kept me on the right path, but after she died, I was so angry at God, at myself. I kept thinking that I could have done better by her. My dad was an alcoholic too. I just gave up, I guess." He looked directly into Chad's eyes. "I regret that. It was wrong."

Chad's throat had closed up. For years he'd hoped to talk, really talk to his dad, and now it was happening. He prayed for the right words. "Dad, did you ever believe in Christ as your Savior?"

"No, I never did, though your mom tried to tell me. That night in the prison, one of the other inmates stood up and yelled over the others who were mostly jeering..."

"What did he say, Dad?" Chad moved closer.

"He yelled, 'Man, you don't have to go to hell. Tell Jesus you're a sinner and that you want Him to forgive you. Tell Him now in your heart. Man, you don't have to go to hell!'"

Then everyone was jeering louder, calling the guy a fool. But...but my cellmate stopped moaning about hell and was quiet. He tried to say something. I leaned forward and I heard, "Jesus." He kind of let go then. I could tell he was dead." He looked up. "It shook me bad. I kept thinking about what the other guy had said about Jesus. I talked to him sometimes. He kept telling me the same."

Chad felt a tremor go through him. "Did you ever talk to Jesus, Dad?"

Slowly, his dad nodded. "I started reading a New Testament a chaplain gave me. I knew I'd get out and I didn't want the drink to get me again. Again I'm sorry, Son, so sorry for how I treated you." His dad swallowed a sob.

Chad gripped his father's hands. "It's time to accept God's forgiveness and forgive yourself. I don't want to keep feeling this distance between us."

"You mean it?"

"With all my heart, Dad."

The two didn't say anything for about a minute. The emotions were too deep for words. Then Chad rose. "I need to get back to town. I have a job to go to. Why don't you rest? I'll be back with groceries later."

Chad's phone rang. He tapped it and listened. "Okay. Thanks." He ended the call. "Shirley wants you to come to supper tonight. She's making a special meal, a celebration that this awful time is over and we're all safe." Would his father refuse the invitation as he had others in the past?

His dad rose. "That sounds nice. What time should I be ready?"

"I'll come and pick you up around five-thirty."

Chad's father surprised him by embracing him. "I'll be ready."

Chad nodded, blinking back tears. He and his dad had taken the first steps toward a new beginning. As he left, Chad's thoughts turned to Jess. Her sweet lips beckoned him even this far apart. Tonight they would talk in the alley on their bench. He smiled, thinking of holding her close.

THE EVENING HAD PASSED SO WONDERFULLY that Jessie felt joy bubbling up inside her. She walked hand in hand with Chad down the familiar alley. However, this time they were walking from Shirley's to their bench. No pizza trade to work on this night. Audra had dropped in with a tray of the most delicious and beautiful cupcakes for dessert. Jessie's diaphragm felt exercised from all the laughing everyone had done around Shirley's table. Then Chad and she had decided to go sit on their bench to finally get some privacy to talk over all that had happened.

However, first they walked to Greg's backyard to greet King. Through the chain-link fence, Jessie slipped him a couple of doggie treats and thanked him again for coming to her rescue. The panic of those few moments tried to surge back but disappeared like smoke on the wind. Joy and gratitude pushed everything bad away.

Soon the two of them sat down on their bench, still hand in hand. At first, they were content to sit and watch the sun sink and the darkness gather. A few fireflies glimmered green on and off.

Finally, Chad cleared his throat.

But before he could say anything, she leaned over and pressed her lips to his. "My heart is full," she whispered when their lips parted. "I told you I was falling in love with you, but now it's final. I'm in love with you."

He said the words back to her.

She smiled and kissed him again. Then she sat back and sighed. "That's all I need right now. We have time. I want to be, I think the word is, *courted*. Let's do all the fun stuff that couples do and just enjoy being together."

"But you are going to be my wife, right?" Chad asked.

She chuckled. "When you get around to proposing, I'll say yes. But let's just enjoy our courtship, and when the time is right, you'll propose. I'll say yes and then plan our wedding. Okay?"

Chad sighed loudly and settled his back against the rough garage wall behind them. "Sounds like a plan. A good one."

They shared a smile and another kiss.

"The last ten days have been horrible, but good has come out of them," she said quietly so as not to disturb the lovely silence. The bar and grill on the main street was closed tonight. "I finally am rid of the past fear. Your dad and you seem to be closer than before, and Dick and Florence are going to marry and share their remaining years."

Chad snuggled another inch closer and rested his face against her hair. "Romans eight verse twenty-eight."

"You got that right," she agreed and kissed him again.

The silence around them continued, just the insects and a car going behind them on the street. It was a time Jessie would never forget. *Thank you, Lord, for everything.*

Epilogue

Three years later

Chad stood very straight as he, along with the other law enforcement graduates, recited the words of their oath. He felt proud in his crisp new uniform and looked forward to starting as one of Harding's deputies tomorrow.

All dressed in their best, Shirley and Tom, Uncle Dick and his wife Florence, and Chad's dad all sat in the same row. Uncle Dick and Florence were living in her house and Chad's dad had moved into the upstairs and was helping them. He was still on the wagon, thank God. And Uncle Dick was renting Chad and Jess his house, the house which they would someday inherit. Uncle Dick had insisted that he wanted Chad and Jess to raise their family there and had made out a new will.

But the very best was gazing at his wife, Jess. Jess had a thriving summer business making artisan bread in Audra's kitchen. Now she was holding their baby girl, just two months old. Or no, now her mother was taking the baby. Jess's parents had decided to retire to the Winfield area and were settling in as eager babysitters. Chad was happy to have them near. They were good people.

For just a second, his dad's gaze connected with Chad's. The pride in that glance burst through Chad like hot sunshine. They'd all come a long way, but now they were here together, all of them. And it was good. *Thank the Lord.*

About the Author

In print for over twenty years, Lyn Cote has written 50+ books. An award-winning author, Lyn writes both contemporary and historical fiction. No matter which kind of story, her brand "Strong Women, Brave Stories" comes through. Her stories always celebrate the triumph of divine as well as human love. She lives in a lakeside cottage in the northwoods of Wisconsin with her comfy husband and adorable cats.

WITHDRAWN